CRY ME A RIVER

DESTINY PARAMORTALS #2

LIVIA QUINN

Praise for Destiny Paramortals

"My new favorite series!" "Okay, I'm hooked, Give me, give me some more!!!" "A bit of magic, a lot of fun and a budding romance!" "Tempest Pomeroy is the best new paranormal heroine of the year!" "OMG, I loved this book. Run don't walk to the buy button." "Destiny. . .is like a mini-vacation from the real world."

If you love Darynda Jones, Eve Langlais or Kristen Painter, you'll like Livia Quinn.

Follow me on: Facebook Twitter Goodreads Instagram Pinterest Bookbub and Amazon

BOOKS BY LIVIA QUINN

Sign up for Livia's spam-free newsletter to receive news and exclusive offers. Click here to sign up

Author's Note

Jack and Tempe have been with me since the summer after Katrina when I was inspired by the quirky characters on my rural mail route *and* the weather in the bayou state. I hope you're enjoying their story. There's a lot to come.

Sign up for my spam free newsletter to get my news and to be included in exclusive giveaways. Follow me on Bookbub and Amazon

liviaquinn.com

Welcome to Destiny, home to the Paramortals since…well, forever… where human neighbors and their new sheriff live alongside shifters, dragons, vampires and a family of djinn.

Just don't tell the humans.

Amid the strange goings on in his new hometown, Sheriff Jack Lang organizes a search for Tempest Pomeroy's brother. Although Jack glimpsed her supposed supernatural talents in the form of lightning bolts aimed directly at him—special effects, had to be—nothing will keep him from doing his job to protect the town's residents, his daughter, and even the trouble-making Tempe.

In the course of the investigation, lies and suspicions cloud their mutual attraction, but Storm Witch Tempe's new ex-Navy pilot beau vows to learn everything about this quirky town.

Everything? Like a massive rumble of thunder, her family secrets—including her brother's djinn nature—shake things up. Sure, Jack may stick around to finish his investigation, but once he knows all about the supernatural aspects of the town…? Well, wouldn't it be just like a man to exit a relationship when he finds out a woman has a few little secrets?

Because in the town of Destiny, the burgeoning, unpredictable supernatural whips up a massive whirlwind of *everything.*

Fans of the Destiny Paramortals say:

"This is my new favorite series!" "WOW…just wow!" "OMG, I loved this book. Run don't walk to the buy button!" "Ok, I'm hooked, give me, give me, give me some more!!"

If you like Darynda Jones, Eve Langlais or Kristen Painter, you'll like Livia Quinn.

CHAPTER 1

A delij k'alant,
cin valo ne kant deligda.

"One meets his destiny
on the road he takes to avoid it."
Ancient Paramortal proverb

Tempe

Monday 4pm "He sounds concussed."

Isn't it just like a man to exit a relationship when he
finds out a woman has a *few* little secrets?

The last time I'd seen my almost boyfriend, Jack Lang,
he'd been out cold on the floor of the Enchanted Glen

clubhouse. Not from drinking, he's the sheriff after all. No, he'd tripped and hit his head when he was... eh... enlightened about Destiny's true *nature*. And about mine.

It was the shock that made him stumble—finding out Destiny is not Mayberry, the quaint ordinary town where he'd planned to raise his daughter, shielded by Plain-Jane humanity from all crime or weirdness. Jack had just gotten his first real look at the underbelly of Destiny, and for now, in his eyes, I'm the *face* of that underbelly. The few tidbits he'd learned earlier at the clubhouse were like snow crystals on the slopes of the Alps, or like raindrops in an ocean of well... extra-normal details.

I tend to think of things in weather terms since I'm a Tempestaerie; some of my human friends just shorten it to storm witch, though I'm not actually any kind of witch.

My name is Tempest Pomeroy, and for nearly twenty years I've denied my heritage because I didn't want to turn out like my mother, Phoebe, or have the problems she and my father, Dutch, had making their relationship work. I thought my father died when I was child, which was the story circulated to the locals, including me. After that, my mother distanced herself from me and my brother, and I was left to raise River, practically by myself.

Last week my brother went missing. Wow, it seems like months have passed instead of just ten days! I discovered a body while delivering mail to the clubhouse, and committed a B&E to retrieve River's Djinni bottle from a locker. The sheriff caught me red-handed and I spent several days trying to convince Jack that I didn't kill the guy, and make him commit resources to the search for my brother. In a matter of days Jack and I went from attraction to suspicion, support to friendship, then romance to *oh-my-god-get-away-from-me* revulsion. I didn't know where we'd go from here once he got the full picture.

He'd found Dylan, my ex-lover and I at the clubhouse sniffing around for clues. Dylan's a Finrir, a shifter-cross between a grizzly and a wolf, so he was *actually* sniffing and tasting. Jack had enjoyed telling me, in front of Dylan, that Dutch was alive. *Is* alive.

It's still shocking to think of it, and it hurts a lot that nearly everyone knew but me. Phoebe, Dylan, and Aurora—my *friend* Aurora, even my brother. I felt betrayed at first but once I heard the reason, I knew I would have to put on my big girl rain boots and adjust.

Jack is an ex-Navy pilot; Dylan said he just needed a little time. He promised to get him to Aurora's tonight and once we finished his indoctrination, he'd either join us, or grab his daughter and take the first jet out of Middle Earth. We don't have time to waste. River's life depends on us.

MONDAY, 4pm Fickle magic

TRUE TO JACK'S Navy call sign, *Laser*, he'd gone straight from unconscious to detective mode.

Dylan called to give me an update as I drove to Aurora's. "Well, he surprised me. He's already asking where you got off to. I guess it's that Navy Commander thing. He picked himself up, crammed that sopping hat on his head and *demanded* we 'get moving on the case now'." Dylan lowered his voice. "He says he wants to know *everything*, and I quote, 'Don't hold anything back'."

I blinked, rubbing my temples with my fingertips. "He sounds concussed." But maybe Marty had been right, maybe there was a chance...

Dylan laughed. "He's a little tougher than I gave him credit for. Anyway, I told him to meet us at Aurora Borealis after he checked in with the Sheriff's Office. I have to check my own messages."

After everything I'd learned about my parents' *grand plan* I had to wonder who would be sending Dylan messages besides his bosses with Universal Mail. Was he in touch with Dutch? I expected answers today after being lied to for so many years. Better yet, I wanted to know exactly where dear old *dad* was.

I ARRIVED at Aurora's at 4:15 and made a beeline back to the workroom while she waited on her customers. Jack's daughter, Jordie, worked here most afternoons but today she had basketball practice.

Now that I had time to think, anger resurfaced. How could Aurora have kept this from me—for nearly my whole life. A sob escaped. I heard glass shatter behind me and turned to see three of the beautiful glass candle shields in splinters on the floor. My breath caught when I realized what I'd done—not on purpose, but this kind of thing had been happening a lot lately. *Menori*, my inner Qi and power center, sensed a presence behind me.

Aurora stood in the doorway. Her expression was sorrowful, her shoulders sagging as she turned, walked to the front door and flipped the sign to *Closed* .

Returning to the workroom she stopped just inside the door. "You're upset with me." I started to turn away, tears welling in my eyes but she tugged me into a motherly embrace. "I'm so sorry, *ha lua*."

Loved one. The words soothed a bit. She pressed a kiss to my hair and rocked me in her arms, while I grieved over the lost years with my parents. It had been nineteen years of feeling like I didn't belong with humans, or supernaturals—like I didn't fit in anywhere. Nineteen years of thinking the breakup of my family was my fault. Nineteen years believing that somehow I'd let everyone down. And hadn't it been confirmed, when all I'd ended up with was a few minimal talents? Mini-rain storms, the ability to lock car doors from twenty feet away, reading an aura that was so obvious even a human could see it. But then, last week I'd saved Mr. Jackson, one of my mail customers, with my zapper. *Talk about a shocker.* (No pun intended.)

Aurora stepped away and gestured to a chair. "I'm glad it's out, Tempe. I can't say it was time because everything we've done was to keep you safe until you went through your quickening, and yet," her hands fluttered up from the table, "here we are—River is in danger, and you still haven't come into your power."

I frowned, feeling raw and confused. "But River knew. I don't understand why you had to keep me in the dark. Maybe it would have made a difference. I might have been able to stop what happened to River—"

"Who knows now, dear heart, but at the time it was the best plan we could come up with. It's common for Paramortals to separate from their offspring during their adolescence. At least, it's what's been done in the past. Your mother and father loved you both, Tempe, and they sacrificed those years with you as well. Phoebe seemed distant and uninvolved after Dutch was... gone, because she had to be. She was supposed to leave Destiny like your father but she couldn't bear to be so far from her children."

Aurora shrugged. "Her presence may have actually kept the plan from working. Until children go through their quickening, they are safe from being tracked by our enemies except through their parents or the speaking of their name by certain guardians."

"Dylan."

She nodded, "Dylan is one."

"Why didn't River ever say anything?"

"Do you remember telling me about River's fourteenth birthday, when he changed and made the wish to see his father again? You thought Phoebe was harsh."

I'd told Aurora about my memory of River's birthday party before I found out Dutch was alive. When my brother made his first wish, to see our father again, my mother had responded with, 'That would be an example of an off-limits or forbidden wish.'

I nodded. It had not been apparent to me before, but that was the day I'd hardened myself toward my mother. River's angst had been obvious. He'd been so young when Dutch left us. The first thing to come across his lips when he got the ability to grant wishes was to see his daddy again, knowing how impossible that was. We'd thought him dead, and then mother had been so cruel to him. I never forgave her for it.

Aurora continued, "That wish caused quite a ruckus. A Djinn isn't allowed to make a personal wish, which was why your mother reacted like she did. She was stunned, worried that their whole plan would be for naught. That's why she resisted leaving.

"River's forbidden wish was excused because he was a newborn Djinn, but it did bring Dutch back from hiding. River's memory had to be washed, which lasted until last week."

I sat back, my mind whirling. River had probably gone looking for answers. And knowing my brother, he would have insisted on telling me. A thought crossed my mind and even with everything that had happened, I rejected it. My parents would *not* have had anything to do with my brother's current predicament, nothing that would have put his life in peril.

I did wonder… "You're not a Guardian?"

"No, just a simple Paramortal godmother," she smiled. "How about a cup of my soothing Borealis tea?"

"I don't know if I'm soothable, but it's worth a try," I said. "Jack and Dylan are going to…" I saw the look on her face. "Oh, you know already."

Aurora nodded. "Dylan called and told me about bringing the good sheriff up to speed."

I'd been furious with Dylan when I found out he'd been an active participant in the conspiracy to keep River and me in the dark until I went through the change. Apparently even our relationship had been orchestrated so Dylan could *baby-sit* me until my Vyal K'allanti—literally the *coming of age*. How mortifying!

It had looked like it was never going to happen, but I'd given Jack a little glimpse of my stormy nature at the clubhouse earlier today. To say he'd been shocked, would be like saying Destiny is a *little* different than the rest of the communities on Storm Lake. Destiny is literally another world. But to Jack's credit, he hadn't run screaming into the night. I chuckled, swiping at my cheeks. "I wish you could have seen his face when Dylan shifted into his beast, but I'm being mean because Jack was operating on overload."

Aurora's right eyebrow angled up. "I doubt that's normal for someone of his experience."

She had that right. Jack had ten years in as a Navy pilot, not to mention his job with the Memphis police and here, as sheriff. He was not one to buckle under stress, at least not the mundane human variety.

My phone vibrated and Dylan's special ring, "Ain't No Way to Treat A Lady" filled the room. Aurora shook her head and I shrugged. What could I say? He'd earned that ringtone. "Yes?" I answered putting him on speaker.

"Lang got a call. He'll let me know when he's done, so stay close to your phone. We'll get this done tonight. I'll call Aurora."

Aurora leaned over to talk into the phone. "No need to contact me, Dylan. I'll be here marking stock and rear-ranging."

"*Zeus' furies!* I was looking forward to getting this over with," I said, after Dylan hung up.

"We need to talk, Tempest." Aurora leaned forward as she weighed her words. Must be bad.

"What did I do?"

She let out an exasperated sigh. "That's what's bothering

me, Tempe. Why do you think you've done anything wrong?"

I shrugged. "Even Jack said it seems like I'm at the center of everything that's happened so far, everything *bad* he meant. I wouldn't be surprised if he—"

"Stop, right there!" I blinked. Aurora's voice cut through the air like a blade. She'd never used that tone with me. "I can see I haven't been a very good godmother." She took my hand and held it tightly. "I want you to really listen to me." This statement was accompanied by one of her piercing looks.

"You're not trying to hypnotize me are you?" I asked.

"No, of course not," she said, flicking that thought away as if it was silly. "Not that I couldn't. Now, don't interrupt, and pay attention." Her eyebrows leveled as she aimed her *Serious Mentor* look at me.

I shut up, expecting a lecture. It didn't turn out that way.

"It's natural for vulnerable children to blame themselves for events that happen, and think there was something they could have done to prevent it. But children are innocents, at the mercy of their caretakers. And even well meaning adults can screw up and make the wrong decisions based on what they deem to be good counsel. Meanwhile their children are left to figure life out the best way they can, especially when they aren't in the loop as you put it. You've heard the old saying, Bel K'jaka?"

I racked my brain for the meaning. "Mm... fickle magic?" I guessed.

"It means literally 'Life is Fickle'."

"Ah." I grimaced, "Stuff happens."

She nodded. "Anytime. Anywhere. Anyhow. Life is one big mountain with a lot of hairpin curves, and we deal with it by accepting who and where we are. You've heard me say this before, Tempe. No matter what's going on around you or who is to *blame*—I hate that word—you are where you are supposed to be, playing your own special part in the universal Qi."

Her aqua gaze got darker, "This shame you feel stems from a false belief that you have control over what happens to you and River."

She was referring to how I'd responded to the planted information about my family, and my feelings toward my mother. Oh, how I'd like the opportunity to make that right. My stomach clenched so hard I nearly doubled over from the ache. I understood. I had been blaming myself for things I had no control over.

"So you're saying..."

"Stop apologizing for who you are, and for *what* you are. Just be *her*. She is exceptional and has a long exciting life ahead of her.

"You have a purpose, Tempe, and it will take shape when it's meant. The Ancients have a saying, 'One meets his destiny on the road he takes to avoid it.' If you're living your truth, you cannot avoid your destiny."

I wanted it to be true. There was something inside that kept me from breaking free... fear, resentment? But the *urge* to let loose was there. It *had* been for quite some time. I'd pushed down even harder in the past week for fear that Jack would see who I really was, and run, but that was probably going to happen anyway. I couldn't worry about that until I found my brother. He was my number one priority... always had been.

"Has my... resistance kept us from finding River?"

"I'm not going there, Tempe. Focus on what *is* and what can be done *now*. The next time you feel *menori* rise, forget the rules; push back the guilt and doubt; and let her rip, baby. Let her rip."

I nodded. "I'll try."

She groaned.

"Okay, I *promise* not to hold back." I risked getting punched and smiled, "Whatever that means..."

CHAPTER 2

TEMPE

5 pm Somebody finally gets it!

CURIOUS ABOUT THE call Jack had responded to, I dialed his number, acting as if nothing had happened earlier.

"I just questioned the woman that filed the complaint against you," he said without preamble, pretending as well.

"Mrs. Karrakas?" The Karrakases lived on the fairway of Enchanted Glen Estates near the clubhouse. She'd filed a complaint a few weeks earlier alleging that I'd stolen a golf club, which she *said* was a gift for her husband. Since it hadn't required a signature, I'd placed it in their open garage near the back door.

"There's something not right about her," Jack said.

"Yes!" I said. *Somebody finally gets it.* "I've been saying that for years. Where did you see her?"

"You'll hear about it before long anyway. Dr. Shone called and needed help with Lancelot."

"Lancelot? Our Enchanted Glen mascot?" Lancelot, a very large, very old alligator lived in the slew near the clubhouse. His slew is the "hazard" at the eighteenth hole. The course had been closed when I discovered the body in a pool of blood in the foyer. Since then we'd learned a lot about the identity of the victim, including that he wasn't human, but we were still in the dark as to who had killed him. Thank the gods, Jack now knew it wasn't me.

"The same. The course was getting ready to open again tomorrow and their new maintenance man spotted Lancelot on the fairway. He was afraid to approach him at first, but when he realized the gator wasn't moving, he called Chris. She hasn't tended to very many alligators so she called the game wardens to get them to transport him to LSU. It seems our Sir Lancelot came down with something. He might have a belly full of golf club."

"My golf club?"

"More specifically, Mr. Karrakas' club. The only identifiable part on it was the head. Lancelot twisted and scarred it up pretty good. He's got a hell of a bellyache. I asked Mrs. Karrakas to identify it, even though I had a pretty good description from McGuinness. It took several of us to load the big boy in the game warden's truck so they could carry him to Baton Rouge."

"Poor baby."

"More like old man. He's got to be at least twenty years old."

"He's probably older than that. I think he was ten when we had the 'Save Lancelot's Slew' campaign. Remind me sometime, I'll show you some pictures."

Silence.

Right. The conversation had been all business, no mention of what happened earlier. He was probably still trying to convince himself it hadn't happened.

"I just left Aurora's. I'm going to run home and change before we meet—"

I realized then, I was speaking to dead air.

As I UNLOCKED my front door, Montana called. "Hey, Temp." She sounded excited. "I think I just saw that construction worker drive up and go into the Wasted Turtle. The description of the truck matched the tag you gave us. Rafe and I had to pick a post in this area so I figured we'd see if anyone showed up. Couldn't hurt, right?"

She was talking about the construction worker who'd been the last one to see my brother, the night before he went missing. Rafe and Montana are EMTs. That's her 'day job' the one humans know about anyway. If you were to meet her under certain conditions, you'd run like hell, especially if you're assaulting a defenseless woman. Rafe is human but enlightened about his partner, and I've always wondered if there wasn't something else going on between them, maybe not romantic because given Montana's "mission", relationships with men are complicated.

"We're *10-11* in the lot across the street and he just drove up. He's got an old beat up red Chevy—you can't miss it—ladder, buckets, a bunch of crap tossed in the bed. We'll try to hang but if we get a call, we'll have to go. You want to head over or do you want me to call Jack?"

"No, I'm on my way. I should be there in less than ten minutes."

Will Crain had been avoiding everyone including Jack, which made his story suspicious. *Menori* roused as I considered how I might convince him to unload his conscience.

Tempe

7:40 pm A friggin' terrible sleuth

I DROVE up beside Montana and Rafe who were still idling and awaiting their next call. The smell of diesel wafted through my window as Montana leaned her head out of the cab of the ambulance. "He's still in there. His truck has a fancy locked toolbox and some other stuff in the back." She pointed to a scuffed up red Silverado parked close to the side exit. "That's it over there."

I was *still* feeling guilty for not realizing my brother was in trouble until I received a call from one of his subcontractors, Max Rutledge, the morning his bottle went missing from our mantel. He'd been irate after River hadn't shown up at the construction site.

My brother is the poster boy for responsibility, and I'd known *then* that something was very wrong. Max had been apologetic after informing me he assumed because of something one of his workers told him that River had overslept, or worse.

Montana asked, "What did this guy tell his boss exactly?"

"He told Max he saw River with a brunette Sunday night 'looking chummy' but he's never answered his phone or been available to sit down with the sketch artist. Jack checked out the address Max had in his records. It's been vacant for a year."

The emergency radio squawked and Rafe listened, then flipped on the siren. "Unit 23 is responding. We're outta here," he said to Montana and Tempe.

"Thank you, Montana," I said as she rolled her window up.

I turned my truck around to face the bar and settled in to wait. The evening had turned cold. The only reason I noticed was that customers exited the bar and then pulled up their collars or hoods and ran for their vehicles. I don't experience temperature changes, unless I concentrate on it, you know, turn on my internal thermometer?

If Jack called, I probably wouldn't tell him about my location, or my intentions. It would make him... unhappy. But I refused to hand over this little recon mission to anyone, because it was the first time I'd had an actual lead I could pursue. Being a law enforcement officer, the sheriff might need a reasonable suspicion of guilt—or whatever they call it—to follow this guy, but all I needed was, well, a bit of gossip and sheer desperation.

As I waited, I remembered what Aurora had said. Phoebe... *Mother* had needed to be near me. My chest burned with guilt at the way I'd condemned my mother for her lack of involvement in our lives. But how could I have known?

Aurora said the plan didn't work, but it seemed to me it had worked fairly well. If it convinced me, it had to have convinced others. The jury was still out on whether I'd been safe because of it, or if my response to their plan kept me from going through my quickening sooner. Who knows what would have happened if Dutch and Phoebe had stayed around to be parents and protect us.

Then there was the situation with Dylan. My teeth nearly cracked when I thought about the morning I'd turned the corner and found him wrapped around one of my female customers—while we were living together. Now that I had the whole picture, I knew he'd definitely been trying to get caught. At the time I'd thought it was a relationship issue—he'd wanted out and was too chicken to tell me, but now I realized it had all been part of the scheme. *Which* just made me even madder with all of them.

I scanned the parking lot. It certainly was a seedy area, the bar backed up to the levee. I'd heard there were plenty of illegal activities being traded out there—everything from sex and drugs to fantasy football bets. Paper debris blew across the gravel lot where it accumulated against the walls and under the porch. Several patrons had already reached their limit and were sleeping it off; one man, snoring loudly on one of the benches, was in danger of toppling onto the pavement. Another half inch and he'd wake up with a concrete headache.

A tap on my window made me jerk to the right. A figure in black stood next to my truck holding something out toward me. A white long stemmed rose. Ducking my head to peer out at the man, I saw that it was Rosco. The African American flower man was thin, but not frail. No matter the weather Rosco dressed in thrift shop elegance—all black except for the threadbare white shirt —black pants, tie, felt hat and a long duster. In the South Louisiana heat and humidity, this made him stand out as he walked the streets with his half dozen long stemmed roses. Few received them, and no one knew why they'd been chosen.

I glanced at the bar as I rolled my window down. I'd never been approached by Rosco before. *Now* would not be a good time for Will to make his appearance. *Menori* swished inside me and I wondered what she sensed. I didn't feel threatened though as I accepted the rose from Rosco. "Thank you." I reached into my ashtray to offer him some change, but when I turned back he was gone. I looked everywhere but he'd slipped away into the dark.

I closed my eyes, breathing in the flower's strong perfume and when I opened them, a man stepped out of the bar, his greasy brown hair and paint-splashed coveralls making me think he was my target. He went straight to the truck with the tools in it. *Yes!* Will Crain. Hopefully he would be a little drunk and a lot careless. He slipped his key into the door lock on the first try— not drunk. Oh, well. I'd have to be very careful. He got in and started the engine. One of his rear taillights was out. That should make him easy to spot from a distance this time of night.

I stayed where I was hunched down behind the wheel and didn't start the engine until he'd turned the corner at the end of the block. I eased out of the hardware store parking lot and drove slowly to the corner. Spotting his single taillight, I pulled onto the road a safe distance behind him.

Why had he given Max Rutledge a phony address? Maybe he was involved with the woman who was seen with River. River's old girlfriend, Paige, had acted very defensive when I'd confronted her on Sunday. My money was on her, but perhaps it was just that I didn't like her. Did Will say he saw River and the "curvy female" to throw suspicion off himself? What if he was directly involved in abducting River? Why though? What would a construction worker have to do with my brother's disappearance? They were both in the construction business, River as an employer... maybe it was personal.

What if Will Crain had River at his place? My breathing quickened and my foot jerked off the gas. *Careful, Tempe, not too close.*

I let a car turn into the lane in front of me knowing I would be able to see when Will turned off. We drove for about four miles before his good blinker light went on and he turned down a road that led to an older section of Destiny where a line of houses and duplexes from the fifties were often rented to farm workers. I slowed at the end of the block and watched his truck drive into the driveway of a dingy white single-family rental.

He got out, walking with exaggerated nonchalance looking for all the world like he hadn't a care. After letting himself into the house, he did the strangest thing. He turned on the light in his front room, and instead of closing his front shades to ensure privacy from prying eyes, he opened the blinds wide so he would be in full view of everyone. Especially me.

As they say in the PI business, I'd been made.

CHAPTER 3

TEMPE

8:15 pm The wienie strikes a deal...

I SAT BACK, stunned. Oh, I wasn't stunned that he'd figured out I was following him, but why make such a point of being seen? At home. Alone.

Now what?

I backed under a tree out of the circle of light cast by a streetlamp and waited, keeping my eyes trained on the house, deciding what my next move should be.

Less than a minute later I heard incessant yapping followed by the sound of toenails on pavement which stopped right outside my door. The yapping continued. Irritated, I stuck my head out the window to see a mottled gray weenie dog grinning up at me. No, I wasn't imagining it. The mutt had frizzy wiry hair that stuck out everywhere and his oddly bent ears looked like a cinch for a malpractice case. The face that stared up at me—the light in those eyes would have been recognizable in any form. He barked again with that weird toothy grin.

"Marty, shut up!"

I popped the door open as quietly as possible, though what did it matter? The stupid dog, er, Imp had put a spotlight on my presence. "Get in here."

His long furry body bounded over my lap to the passenger seat. He didn't change forms though.

"What do you want?" I wanted to shake him until his phony hotdog hairs fell out. "Is it River? Have you found him?" My voice had risen.

In a blink Marty changed, plopping his butt down on the seat, the wrinkly skin above his eyes turning down. "I'm sorry, Tempest. I didn't mean to worry 'ya."

"So you don't know anything?"

He shook his head. "It's as if he—well, I don't know. I've never *not* been able to contact him before."

"So what's with the Dachshund getup? And why didn't you pick one of those pretty classic ones?"

"Oh, you like the shorthairs better?" And just like that, sitting before me was a beautiful little black and tan, the expression on its doggy face so sweet, for a moment I forgot who I was talking to. "You like?" he asked, lifting a paw and stroking his "brow".

"Look, you've got to go…"

"Okay, okay. I overheard one of the girls at the vet the other day—"

The other day being the day Dr. Shone had called to tell me my Pomeranian was disrupting her clinic. I don't have a Pom, and neither do I have a Dachshund, but Marty had agreed to take on a more human friendly form. "And…?"

His voice rose excitedly, "She said there's going to be a Wiener Derby at Mardi Gras this year. I wanna go." He jumped straight into the air, nearly bumping his head on the roof, wiggling his long weenie backside, the tail going *swat, swat* against the vinyl seat.

"What's that got to do with me, Marty?"

He plopped down on the seat exasperated. "I need a parent… to fill out the forms and handle me, Tempest. Pleeeease, I don't have anyone else to ask." His head sank down against his skinny black chest then he tilted it strategically and looked up at me with sorrowful dark eyes.

Tires crunched on the pavement outside. A *fine* sleuth I'd make. I'd missed Will Crain's exit from his house. He was going somewhere. I had two choices. I could follow him, or… I had a sudden inspiration. No one should be surprised.

I turned to Marty. "Okay, I'll make you a deal." He gave me a wide toothy smile and yipped as I watched one taillight disappear from view.

I was going to be in so much trouble if anyone found out about this.

Tempe

8:45pm And another plan bites... the dust?

I DON'T KNOW why Marty didn't just change into Imp form and travel in a more efficient manner. He seemed to get a kick, or a challenge, out of using those short stubby legs to bounce along beside me, jumping over roots and downed trees as we made our way through the strip of woods to the back of Will's house. I know what you're thinking—another B&E. *Well,* you'd be right. Somehow it just didn't seem wrong to try to get a heads up on a criminal. Besides in my case, with *menori* operational, I didn't think there'd be any breaking going on. That was one talent that I could depend on.

But when we arrived at the back door, no talent or tools were necessary. The door was open, the only thing standing between us and a little stealthy scavenging was an old wooden, *unlocked* screen door. I smiled. Then I realized if he'd left the house open he was probably on a short trip to the closest convenience store for beer. "Come on, Marty, we have to be fast."

He jumped through the hole in the screen as I reached for the door, at the last minute using my t-shirt around the handle to open it.

The place reeked of cigarettes and trash. My eyes watered as the pungent odors assaulted my highly reactive senses. I let *menori* off her leash and began checking the rooms. Number one on my list was to see if my brother was here, though I already knew from the way Will had left the house open and left himself in full view earlier, River wasn't being kept here. *Menori* was having a hard time picking up anything concrete. The foul smell of trash, smoke and general pollution of the property was interfering with her accuracy.

I didn't really know if *menori* was male or female, but I couldn't quite wrap my mind around a male Qi living inside of me. So until I knew for sure, I was believing it was a 'her'. Or it could be an it. Why had I never given it more thought, and why now? *Zeus' hairy bum*, Tempe. Get busy.

The bedrooms were spare except for the one where Will slept which was a wreck. The whole place was a house-keeping nightmare. When Will did move out, the only way to clean it would be to call in a HAZMAT team. A sound filtered through my thoughts and Marty growled low in his faux doggie throat. A vehicle was approaching. Already?

I ran to the window in the bedroom that faced the front yard. Sure enough, Will was returning. I caught a glimpse of him in the cab talking on his phone and hissed, "Out, Marty. *Now*." I took one more, quick glance around the living room and followed him out the back door, pushing the screen shut as I heard the rumble of Crain's Chevy pulling into the driveway.

We took off through the woods, being as quiet as possible while making quick progress, but by the time we made it to the street at the edge of the woods, we were both breathing hard. I bent over to get my breath, heaving and taking in great gulps of air. Marty whined, then yipped.

Jack

"What size jumpsuit do you wear?"

If I ADMITTED I was getting used to Tempe's shenanigans, I'd also have to admit to some sense of normalcy, to accepting the craziness around her as something I could deal with, some day.

Earlier today I'd been ready to get the hell out of Destiny but my job had... no, that was bullshit. My job wouldn't have kept me here for longer than it took to grab Jordie and put my foot to the pedal. It was Tempe. Damn it. She'd gotten under my skin. I couldn't help it.

I captured a mental video of the sight in front of me—Tempe, red hair flying, those long legs pumping, her tennis shoes slapping the street as she cast a furtive glance over her shoulder as she made the dash for her truck. A black Dachshund bounced along beside her, its tongue lolling out until he got a glimpse of me and his hind end hit the pavement. Tempe bent over, one hand on her stomach, the other palm on her knee. Her shoulders heaved as she gasped for breath and colorful strands of hair waved around her calves. "Whew, I'm out of shape, Marty."

The dog looked at me and yipped again, his hassling tongue dripping saliva.

Tempe looked up for a second, then slowly rose from her stoop.

"Zeus' bumbling cousin!" Her eyes widened when she saw me, then narrowed. Looking off, she tried for nonchalance, as if hightailing it out of the woods like a wildfire was on her ass was something anyone would ignore.

"What size jumpsuit do you wear?" I asked.

Breathing hard, she frowned and gasped, "What are you talking about?"

"I figure we might as well get your prison outfits ordered in your preferred size. If you keep this up, you're going to wind up there eventually and then they may only have XLs." She knew what I was referring to. I'd found her breaking into the clubhouse locker to get River's amphora the first day I'd met her. And after I ordered her to stay away from my crime scene, she'd snuck back in at four in the morning to search the grounds.

"How do you do that?" She planted her fists on her hips and frowned. "Did you plant a tracking device on me or something?"

"As if I needed one. You couldn't hide your feelings unless you wore a black sack over your head, and your intentions are as predictable as the full moon." I softened my voice, "Especially when it comes to your brother."

Her eyes blinked suddenly and she turned away but I recognized the slump for what it was. Defeat. Whatever her plan had been, she'd failed.

"What happened?"

Tempe

8:57 pm One B&E away from a permanent vacation

HE WAS *ALWAYS* TURNING up when I was in, um, a predicament, mostly of my own making. Like my first Breaking and Entering...

He said, "In this case, I happened to be driving by the Wasted Turtle when I saw you talking to Rafe and Montana. I was about to come over and ask what you were up to when Will Crain walked out of the bar, and you pulled out behind him. So I followed you."

"You foll—" I was a friggin' *terrible* sleuth. Not only had I been made by the person I was tailing , but I'd also missed the sheriff's big SUV on my tail.

"What are you doing here, Tempe?" He looked down at the wienie dog by my feet, whose head went back and forth following our conversation. Jack seemed impressed with my training skills. "I thought you had a Pomeranian. Who's this little fella?" He leaned over toward my "dog" and Marty darted away. Some protector he turned out to be.

"He... belongs to a friend." Jack was right. I'm a terrible liar. "I thought it might be good to bring him along, in case..."

"In case someone surprised you, like the home owner for instance? I can see how well that worked out for you. Look, you could have screwed up any chance we had of tying Crain to Paige or River, if he's involved."

I looked down the street to where my truck was parked. A streetlamp illuminated Marty as he wagged his tail and looked up at Jack, grinning. Changed his mind, huh. *My hero*, the look clearly said. Jack bent over and picked Marty up.

"You're a cute little fella. It's a good thing you don't like to bark."

"You should have been here thirty minutes ago—oh, you were." I stared at him. "If you were here, why did you allow me to walk up in there?"

He grinned, his broad white smile gleaming in the glare

of the streetlight. "Hell, I just wanted to see what you were going to do. I had a bet with Ryan that you had your burglar tools on you."

"Funny, ha-ha. What am I, some kind of law enforcement science project?" Ryan is Jack's deputy and his wingman from the Navy. He followed Jack to Destiny after getting out of the service. He is *not* in-the-know about Destiny's *other* side.

"I sent Ryan after Will when he left. I was beginning to think I was going to have to distract Crain if you didn't get out of there. I told Ryan you were hell with door locks. Is that how you got in?"

"I just walked in the back door. It wasn't locked."

He handed Marty to me. "Don't you have a leash for this mutt?" Marty growled. "Easy there, boy, no offense meant. As I was about to say before your 'guard-dog' chastised me, I'm going to go talk with Mr. Crain before we lose him again. It won't hurt if you want to come along. You weren't in there long enough to see anything were you? Or find anything?"

"No. But you'd better have all your shots before searching that place."

"I have to have reasonable cause to even request a warrant to search, but I'm working on it. Don't blow it. I'm going to pull around. Follow me. And leave your little buddy in the car."

CHAPTER 4

TEMPE

9:15pm Big fat juicy lies

JACK TURNED down Crain's street and drove up behind the pickup in the driveway, blocking it. He got out and told me to stay in my truck until he signaled that it was safe.

Safe? I hadn't thought of that. The guy might have been waiting on me to come to the door. He could have been sitting there looking innocent, baiting me. I guess I needed more practice at this.

Jack knocked on the door. I saw Will get up from the chair as Jack walked up the sidewalk to the porch. Be careful, Jack... The door opened and I could hear the conversation from my parking spot near the curb.

"Sheriff, what can I do for you? '

"Are you Will Crain?"

"That's me," the guy said, a little too cheerfully, and loudly.

"I'd like to ask you a few questions, Mr. Crain."

"Why sure, Sheriff. Why don't you and the lady come in?"

I saw Jack hesitate for a split second, as surprised as I had been. He assessed it for some kind of trap. Finally, he called out, "Tempe, why don't you join Mr. Crain and me?"

I scrambled out of my truck, locking it—with my key, instead of my zapper— and walked toward the house. Jack's narrowed gaze told me he'd been watching.

"Dispatch, I'm at 1022 Oak St. interviewing a subject." Jack spoke into the radio on his lapel. A safety measure, I presumed, as well as to make a point. *We may be coming inside, but others know where we are so don't try anything.*

We stepped into Will's house and the smell of stale cigarettes and trash once again assaulted my nostrils. It was worse than the unventilated smokers lounge at the Crossroads Truck Stop. I wouldn't put *menori's* gag reflex to the test unless I got some signal from Jack.

Will offered us seats on the couch and Jack accepted but sat on a chair, one leg propped on the other across from Will. I just couldn't do it. I stood leaning as casually as I could against the grimy couch. Misshapen with deep depressions in the cushions, and discolored, it was the ugliest piece of furniture I'd ever seen.

"Mr. Crain, I've been trying to get in touch with you for a week. Mr. Rutledge had a different address on file for you."

Will just shrugged. "Well, I've lived right here for the last three months. I don't know why he didn't have the right address."

"Uh-huh. Any reason why you didn't return any of my phone calls?"

"I've been busy working. Twelve to fourteen hour days don't leave much time for chatting."

Jack's aura turned a few vibrant shades of red at Crain's words and his shoulders bunched.

"Well, Will. Do you mind if I call you Will? I'm surprised you have such a blasé attitude about what we, that's the sheriff's department and Ms. Pomeroy's family, thought was important information."

For the first time, Will looked a little nervous. I could imagine. I'd been the recipient of that hard silver stare. It was unnerving.

"So, let's 'chat'." Jack laid one wrist over the other casually and leaned forward. I expected him to flip out his trusty notepad, but I'd suspected all along he didn't really need it to remember details. Crain stared back at him as if hypnotized.

Jack said, "I understand you were at the Wasted Turtle last Sunday night. How often do you visit that particular establishment?"

Will blinked. "Uh, every now and then. What difference does that make?"

"Now don't get defensive, Will. I'm just trying to establish your veracity as a witness."

"O…kay."

"What time did you arrive?"

Will pretended to think hard then looked directly at Jack. "I think it was about four."

"And what time did you leave?" Jack asked.

"Now that I don't know exactly, but I believe it was before midnight." Once again, he made an exaggerated face. Jack didn't seem bothered by the man's obvious stall tactics.

"You told your boss you saw River at the bar that night. What time was that?"

Crain scratched his cheek and searched his pockets for another cigarette. "I don't know. I'd had a few by then. But he left before I did."

"Did you know the woman with River?"

"Nope. Never seen her before but she was *hot*."

Jack pulled out *the notebook*. "Can you give me a description besides *hot*?"

Crain inhaled deeply then blew a long plume of smoke into the air. Pretending to bring the woman into focus, he closed his eyes, "Um, sorta tall, brunette, tight jeans, built like a..." he grabbed his chest with both hands, cigarette dangling until he caught Jack's look and dropped his hands to his lap, glancing over at me, "uh, big up top, 'ya know."

"Eye color, distinguishing characteristics?"

I rolled my eyes. This was absurd.

"Hmm, it's just not coming to me right now."

Jack put his pad back in the pocket of his coat and asked, "What did you mean when you told Max they looked 'chummy'?"

"Well, River was about three sheets and leaning on her, feeling her up, 'ya know, and she was giggling and supporting him... they were kind of supporting each other."

Thunder rolled through the room, rattling the dishes in the sink, shaking Will's ashtray.

Will grabbed the arms of his chair, eyes wide.

Jack gave me a sideways glance.

"Sounds like more rain," I said and shrugged. *Menori* stirred again and the floor under our feet shook with another low rumble of thunder. I clamped my teeth together so I didn't interrupt to say that my brother was a gentleman. He wouldn't be "feeling a woman up" in a bar in full view of the other patrons.

Jack swung his head back to Will concentrating on his next question, "Have you seen either Mr. Pomeroy or the woman he was with since that day?"

"No." A quick, short answer and a head shake.

"Do you have any idea where we might find River? Or what might have happened to him?"

There was the slightest of hesitations and a twitch of one eyelid. I was sure Jack noticed. "Look, I'm trying to help. I told you he went home with that woman at the bar. Why don't you find her and ask her?"

Jack smiled that reptilian smile of his. "Oh, I will. You can count on it. I need you to come down to the station tomorrow. I'll have a deputy pick you up in the morning at seven."

"Why? Are you arresting me?"

Jack gave a mock look of concern. "Have you done something I should arrest you for, Will?"

"Uh," he licked his lips, doing his best to look abashed. "No, of course not. But uh, why are you sending a deputy to pick me up? I could drive over and then I could leave from there for work."

Sounded reasonable to me, but not to Jack.

"Oh, no, Will. I can't have you using your gas when you'll

be helping us out. What kind of mileage do you get in that junk heap outside anyway, eight MPGs? Nah, it would cost you a fortune to drive to New Orleans in that thing."

"New Orleans!"

"Sure, Will, and I'll even buy you lunch. You want to help Ms. Pomeroy find her brother don't you?"

Will looked at me. I spread my lips into a phony smile.

"Well... sure."

"We'll clear it with your boss, Will. Would that be Max?"

"Hmm, I... no, you don't need to do that. I'll just call in sick."

Jack suddenly pulled a convenience store coffee cup from the inside of his jacket and extended it to Crain, clearing his throat. "Could I trouble you for a cup of water? I'm parched." He made an inane attempt at a cough.

Will obliged him and we sat in silence until he returned, Jack's lips curving up in a crooked smile. What was he up to?

Will handed the cup to Jack.

"Thanks." Jack rose and I followed suit. "All right then. Dream up a nice clear image of the woman with River because you'll be meeting with a forensic artist tomorrow. We appreciate your cooperation. The deputy will be here at seven sharp. Have a good night."

Crain nodded but his eyes narrowed.

I couldn't help it; I called up a few negative ions and sent them in Will's direction. As we walked down the steps I heard him yelp.

Outside, Jack said mildly, "Couldn't help yourself, could you?" He walked me to my car where the darkness hid us from Will's view. "Did that world-class sniffer of yours detect anything in there?"

"Besides cigarette smoke?"

"Cigarettes, weed, probably Meth…" He tossed the water onto the grass and whipped a plastic bag out of his pocket, carefully placing the cup inside. "But what I detected most of all was big fat lies."

CHAPTER 5

JACK

9:25 pm Lord Sheriff of the "Rings"

I WALKED her to her truck, the shadows shielding us from view. I glanced at the house. Crain had closed his blinds and turned the light out in the front room. "Looks like Mr. Crain decided he wants privacy all of a sudden."

I placed my fingertip under her chin and tilted her face where I could her eyes in the moonlight. "Good job, Deputy. We've got our first real lead." It was habit to scan the street, searching for anything out of place. But tonight it was more of an attempt to keep from answering a silent call, the pull I felt between us. Her eyes had that sparkling meteor shower thing going on in them. I was never sure what caused it. Emotion? Anger?

Desire? Or was another storm brewing in that pretty head?

"Was that you making the earth move in there?" I asked. I was mesmerized by those eyes. When her mouth opened and she seemed to be at a loss for words, I couldn't help myself. I knew I shouldn't scratch that itch, but I wanted to taste her again. I could call it curiosity, but it was more than that. Desire for her would not let me go until I had just one taste.

I told myself *just one more kiss* and I'd get the urge out of my system but... when my mouth closed over hers there was a soft exhalation, a sigh of satisfaction—mine, or hers? She wasn't indifferent, grabbing my hair with her hands and turning the kiss more than I'd intended. Her tongue dueled with mine and as I pressed my body into hers, her hips pressed against me. God, she tasted sweet and I realized my curiosity wasn't about to be tamed with this limited exploration. How had I forgotten where we were? I ended the kiss and heard another little moan of need escape her.

I backed away not knowing quite what to say. My thoughts were all tangled up with a gut feeling I couldn't nail. It was something essential. Still, *this* was definitely not the place and with everything going on, it wasn't the time. We had another question and answer session to get to, and I wasn't at all sure how that would go.

She frowned, "What is it?"

I shook my head and cast a glance over at the house.

"Why don't you head over to Aurora's? I'll be along after I check with dispatch."

She nodded and I waited while she got in her truck. "Where's your dog?"

"I'm not sure, and I told you he's not mine." She shrugged. "I'll see you at Aurora's," she said but didn't pull away, instead waiting, perhaps trying to figure out what I was thinking.

Finally she gave up, and as she drove away I was still standing there, trying to figure it out myself.

I'D NEVER FELT MORE CONFLICTED in my life.

Thinking back to the first day when I met Tempe, I'd used words like trouble magnet, flake, liar, thief—and more. Then I learned that she was crazy with concern for her brother; stressed over her work situation and my accusations. In addition to that, her mother had gone AWOL.

A few days later, she heard I was investigating a body that had been discovered down near Amity. She'd been fearful that it might have been River and had tried to get information from her ex-lover, the Postal Inspector who'd taken advantage of her vulnerability. I'd gone straight from the scene to tell her the good news and found her and Diablo in a lip lock—that's how I'd thought of McGuinness back then since he'd reminded me of a dangerous gunslinger in a cheesy western.

She'd stormed off... appropriate... and I recognized my feelings as jealousy. I followed her to her mother's house to apologize and found her emotionally and physically drained. It was probably the low point of her life—until the next day, when I slammed her with the news about her father being alive. Oh, I'd been so cocksure I was getting somewhere with that strategy. Now, I watch her reaction over and over in my head and feel an ache in my chest—regret, guilt? There was *a great deal* I didn't know.

I'm not sure how I feel about Tempe being... what did she call it... well, being *not*normal—I hated to use the "A" word but it's how I'd come to look at life since Georgeanne. It was probably time to start accepting the fact that I wasn't going to find *Normal*, USA. And wasn't normal just another word for boring?

When I chose a career in the Navy, I hadn't been interested in simply moving one foot in front of the other, plodding through the minutia of life, or the service. No, I'd squeezed every facet of life, every iota of danger, every thrill from my experiences, including those things that were new and strange to me, *especially* the ones that were strange. Where had that side of my personality gone? What had I become? I might be experiencing PTSD, but the post traumatic stress wasn't from the service. It had happened because of my marriage to Jordie's mother and what she'd put us through.

One thing you could say about Destiny, and Tempe Pomeroy, there was never a dull moment. AND YET,

DESPITE THE CRAZINESS, THIS PLACE HAD CARVED A PLACE IN MY HEART. You don't become a Navy pilot if you enjoy being bored. *But remember Jack, this wasn't about you.* No, my reasons for choosing Destiny had all been about my daughter, making sure she would be safe.

I turned into the S.O. thinking about Jordie. She felt at home in Destiny. She and Tempe had really hit it off, and she had yet to meet any supernatural creatures. *Yet.* Maybe she wouldn't have to. Hmm, notice I hadn't called Tempe a creature. McGuinness... I shivered... *now, there was a creature.*

Peggy was working long hours. She handed me a note from Ryan when I walked through the door and followed me into my office.

"You had a call from Del Burke over in Larue. She said it was important."

I stretched my legs out under my desk and dialed the Larue police officer.

"Burke," came a crisp female voice.

"Jack Lang here, from Destiny. I understand you have some info for me."

"Yes, I saw your inquiry come across my desk about Will Crain. He was a resident here for about six months, two years ago. The contract on the apartment showed two lessees, his name and a Paige Whyte."

Burke spelled it P-a-y-g-e W-a-y-t-t. I smiled. *Gotcha.* "I can't tell you how glad I am you paid attention, Burke. That's the break I was waiting for."

"Glad I could help. I'll fax over a copy of the lease. We've added some volunteers, mail carriers mostly, that we've assigned to check abandoned dwellings. I'll keep you updated." She hung up.

"We got him, Peggy. He was on a lease with Paige last year in Larue. Get a warrant to search Crain's place. We'll do it in the morning while he's in New Orleans with the sketch artist. I don't want him to get wind of our interest and run before he can lead us to Paige."

"Yes, sir."

I got Ryan on the phone and advised him of the latest. "Sit on him, and be real careful not to be seen. We can't afford to spook him until we find River's whereabouts. I'll have a warrant by morning."

"So you think River's been kidnapped?" Ryan asked. I'd almost forgotten he wasn't in on all the… insider details. I'd have to play this by ear.

"Yeah, I'll fill you in later. What did you find out from the warden?"

"*That* was weird. He says he doesn't remember anyone incarcerated there by the name of Dutch Pomeroy. We checked the computers—nothing. What would be the likelihood that he was there under an assumed name?"

I thought about that. If he was there to keep his enemies from finding him, it was highly possible. *Or everything could have been erased.* "I don't know. Peggy talked to the warden. She saw the records showing his name. Forget that for now. Our priority is to find River, and keep Tempe from suffering the same fate. She and McGuinness think whoever has River may be planning on eliminating him soon."

Or take his power, I thought. I shook my head. Dylan had called the beings like him and the Pomeroys 'people of power". Hmm, *P.O.P*, I like it. *POP* made it sound less like I was living in the next "Rings" movie.

CHAPTER 6

TEMPE

10pm Do not call me any of those ridiculous 'P' names!

AURORA'S special tea sat untouched in front of me.

A coded sequence of knocks on the rear door announced the arrival of Dylan followed a few minutes later by Jack. Aurora placed cups of her special concoction in front of each of them.

Jack looked at his suspiciously while Dylan slugged his down.

Something had been bothering me ever since the scene at the clubhouse. "Did you know about Dutch?" I asked Aurora.

"You mean where he was? Of course. Your mother

contacted me before she left town. Nigel and Sam," she saw my frown, "the other two protectors, didn't give her a choice about leaving." She glanced over at Dylan, passed the baton.

Dylan uncrossed his arms and leaned forward. "This is a power play, Tempe. The more distant the targets are from each other right now, the better. Yours and River's safety is our number one priority." He went quiet frowning at me.

"What?"

"Didn't you know, in *here*," he tapped his chest, "that Dutch was alive? I've heard the way you described his 'leaving'. I've even heard you say that maybe he ran off and left Phoebe because… she was a 'flake'."

Dylan winced as the words crossed his lips. "Your parents are good friends of mine and the worst part for me was listening to people scorn your father and cast blame on Phoebe, especially you."

Aurora started to speak but Dylan held up his hand. "You know that's not true now, right? The whole ordeal was necessary. He reached across the table for my hand. "It was also unfair and… painful, I know." This was more emotion and honesty than I'd gotten from Dylan in my entire life.

And about damn time, I thought, looking at his hand like it was a poisonous viper. I slammed my cup down. "Well, I'd have known that, and I would have had a rela-tionship with my mother like you both, and River, if I'd been told. *Zeus' blazing balls!"* I marched to the other side of the room—knew I was throwing a tantrum but I was just so…

"Duck!"

Dylan shoved Jack to the floor and Aurora dove behind the counter as electric blue arcs of fire lashed around me. I held my arms out in front of me as the zigzags of blue and white wavered along my limbs, like they were awaiting direction...

My hair flayed around my head like whips. I saw shock on Jack's face and immediately experienced shame at what he was witnessing.

The conversation with Aurora about *letting go* floated around me on a diaphanous cloud. The charged currents dispersed, as quickly as they'd soared, leaving only the slick floor and the pungent scent of burnt oxygen.

"You can get up now, Jack," I said, wishing I was anywhere else. Jack eased into his chair as Dylan and Aurora exchanged glances.

"What? Surely, you've seen a crazy, mad Paramortal child throw a temper tantrum."

"I thought you were finally going to do it, P…"

"Don't!" I glared at Dylan. "Just don't for whatever reason call me one of those riciculous 'P' names."

Aurora was thoughtful. She shushed Dylan with a look.

"Tempe, you've been fighting this for so long, I haven't a clue *what* is going to set *menori* loose. I'm a bit concerned that you won't be able to control it when it does."

Menori is what we in Tempesaerie land call the "breath of life". It... she found River's amphora in the locker, even though I'd told Jack I'd smelled it.

Even then, he didn't buy it.

Dylan made a motion with his hand like you'd use to tell a dog to stay. His bossy autocratic ways were starting to irritate me. Had he always been like that? "Sit down, Tempe, before you blow the windows out for no good reason."

Jack spoke impatiently, "If what you've said about Dutch is true, why did he choose now to get out of prison?"

Jack

What is Saturday, the pumpkin hour?

DYLAN SAID, "He's coming for his family. He's uniquely qualified to help find River."

Tempe looked at Dylan, the expression on her face so hopeful, it made my chest hurt.

"Why is that?"

Tempe looked anxiously back at me. She put her hand on my arm, but I didn't respond. I needed to concentrate. Looking resigned, she let go and asked, "Do you remember I told you about River being a Djinni?"

"Yeah…"

"My father is Djinn as well."

"And very powerful," Dylan said.

"Are we talking genie… like the one on that old TV show? Granting wishes…like that?"

Tempe nodded. "Just like that."

"Well, not exactly," Dylan interjected. "River doesn't look nearly as cute in his Djinni outfit."

"Dylan!" Tempe punched him in the arm.

It was all starting to sink in. I'd known there was something off about the murder, and about the town, but I'd avoided the truth, because I didn't want to see it. Deluded myself into thinking it was what I'd wanted it to be, because—and this was the irony—it was *where* Jordie and I wanted to be. Despite its craziness, this place had carved a place in our hearts. Something shifted within me at that realization.

"Go on," I said, hoping they'd go into detail, because I had no clue what questions to ask.

Dylan crossed his arms and sat back. "You're aware now that River's amphora is critical to sustaining his life force. He would not be voluntarily separated from it and can't live much longer without being reunited with a proper vessel."

That's what she'd been hiding from me early in the investigation. Well, naturally. She'd known I wasn't ready, might never be. "So..." my deductive reasoning was starting to function again, "...why would someone want River? And if he was in trouble, why did his mother take a hike?"

"My main regret in all of this is the way you humans have made Phoebe out to be some kind of monster," Dylan said with a growl. He scrubbed his face with long fingers and sighed before settling into his narrative.

"Okay, Lang, remember we talked about people of power? You know about the bad guys, or one faction of them—the variants. The good guys," he spread his hands out presumably to include himself, "are called Paramortals. Dutch, Phoebe and River are Paramortals, along with a few other folks in Destiny."

"You and Aurora?" I asked Dylan.

He nodded.

"And Montana and Katerina—" Tempe said.

I grunted. "I knew there was something strange about 0007. All right." I blew out a long breath. "What about these enemies you mentioned?"

Dylan said, "They take on many forms. Variants, fae, both corporeal and incorporeal. That's blooded and, er...not."

I twitched.

Dylan waved his hand, "Don't go there right now. Stay with me. Dutch and Phoebe knew when they had children they would have to part from each other and from their offspring—sorry—children in order to protect them, until they went through their *Vyal K'allanti*."

I raised my hand, but Dylan said, "Hold on, I'm getting to it. The *Vyal K'allanti* is the quickening of power in a new Paramortal, which River went through at fourteen. Tempe, Phoebe and I were there. He was presumably able to protect himself after that. Dutch went to prison because there, in that particular facility, behind iron bars, he was undetectable from our dark fae enemies."

He anticipated my next question, "Fae as in faerie, and not like in the movies."

My mind leaped to what Ryan had said. "Did it make him invisible as well?"

Dylan nodded. "Very good, Jack."

Tempe turned to Dylan, "So why now? Why did Dutch choose now to leave his refuge if I haven't changed?"

Changed? My heart started palpitating. I thought I could hear it squawking, *Warning, meltdown.* Just when I thought they couldn't dump more weird, queer and bizarre facts on me, the words, "you humans", had just been delivered to my brain. Meaning Dylan and Tempe... "Oh, sh—"

"I see you're getting the big picture, Jack." Dylan sat

back rubbing his neck. His hand plopped down on the table, "Finally."

He turned to Tempe. "The reason I've always called you those ridiculous, albeit *affectionate* nicknames is because as a guardian I wasn't supposed to address you by your real name and risk our enemies tracking you here through that connection. Think about how difficult that was for me for the last several years."

A typical McGuinness rationalization, I thought. And were we really concerned about how difficult things had been for him? I wanted to plant my fist in that clueless jaw of his.

Tempe spoke after absorbing his words. "I can't believe I didn't notice. You only called me by name to my face once—recently."

Dylan's eyebrow hiked, "The night I kissed you." He looked over her shoulder at me. "And we were rudely interrupted."

I said, "And that is what triggered Dutch's release, or escape, or whatever?" I leaned back balancing on two chair legs, tapping my middle finger on the arm of the chair and listening as everything added up.

"So it is my fault," Tempe said, "because I've been in denial about taking my power. That's right, isn't it, Dylan?"

Dylan looked down at the table.

"It's the reason River was taken and Phoebe was forced to leave," Tempe pressed.

"I blame myself," Dylan said. "I told you I was sorry about how we broke up, but I thought it was worth a try to shock you into your quickening. It didn't work, and then you stayed away from me so I had no influence with you. If anything, it just made you more... resistant to the change."

Everything they said went into my cop centrifuge and it spit out a conclusion I didn't like. "They're coming for her," I said, and somehow, I didn't think she'd be able to defend herself from the bad guys Dylan described with baby thunderstorms and mini lightning bolts.

Dylan said, "*And* for River, if we don't find him first. Alive, they would be of more use as leverage, but dead means, bottom line—fewer Paramortals to contend with." Tempe looked at me, then at Aurora.

Dropping the chair back onto the floor with a thump I addressed Tempe. "You were convinced Paige was involved in this."

"I still am," she said confidently.

"You were right, and I think I just got proof. I got a call from a police department on the east end of the lake. Will and Paige were on an apartment lease together two years ago. They tried to hide it by spelling her name a different way. Now we've connected them."

"That's great!" She jumped out of her chair and paced. "So can you arrest him and make him talk?"

"I *get* that time is of the essence, Tempe, but this isn't the Spanish inquisition. We have to follow a few rules. The plan is still to pick him up in the morning and carry him to New Orleans to see the sketch artist. He may trip up somehow, but while he's gone we're going to search his house. Maybe we'll get lucky and turn up something to locate Paige. We're searching property and rental records but so far nothing's popped."

Dylan said, "Keep me in the loop, but we need to discuss our emergency plan in case we don't find him by Saturday."

"What is Saturday, the pumpkin hour?"

"River's force will expire," Dylan said succinctly.

Tempe choked out, "My brother will die."

The room was silent for several seconds. I reached toward Tempe but Dylan put his hand on her shoulder and patted her back.

Eyes narrowed at him, I asked, "Is Paige a POP?"

They all looked at me quizzically. Dylan frowned, "What's a POP?"

Tempe said to Dylan, "I get it. Jack's come up with an acronym from our talk at the clubhouse—People of Power—POP." Turning to me she said, "Paige is a borderline Tempestaerie. She couldn't do anything but predict humidity—and *that* only when her hair gets frizzy."

There was another word I'd heard Aurora use. "What is Air and… too?"

Aurora said, "*Aretuu* means 'enemy of all', in our language it literally means 'I am hate'."

"So these *Aretuu*, are they the ones who are after Dutch? The ones you think took River?" My head was swirling with new facts. *Facts?* "What makes a POP a Paramortal, anyway? And is every city in this country full of you people?"

Tempe swung toward me. "You people?" *Uh-oh.* She was getting irritated again. "Thanks a lot, Jack. I suppose the reason you're asking is that you're still contemplating some mythical safe existence. Was Memphis any more desirable than Destiny? I'm surprised a man with your experience believes there's some Sitcom-esque place with no issues out there where you can raise a teenager in a bubble. Get real."

I sighed. I was out of my depth, but I *was* trying. I persisted, "So… to clarify… Paramortals are *not* human?"

Tempe muttered, "He's ignoring me."

Dylan said, "Not really. Calm down." He plucked a piece of paper from Aurora's printer and leaned forward. "I'll try to make this as simple as possible. To answer the first question, most places have few of what *you* might call extra-humans—those who have some hereditary Paramortal qualities that exclude them from mere-mortal*ness*—hell, this isn't simple. We've created more nicknames in the last twenty-four hours than in all of history. Some Paramortals-to-be may even seem totally human until they find themselves in the middle of their quickening. Then it's kind of an *aha* moment." Dylan grinned. Tempe rolled her eyes.

"Paramortals is a catch-all term that includes all supernatural species, even a few human hybrids under the blood pact. They exist everywhere, but we have more than our share here in Destiny because of a super pulse of leylines running through the West end of Storm Lake."

Dylan drew a fairly decent approximation of Storm Lake, placing the leyline from northwest of Hugo, around the western shore, and adding a line from Destiny east to the middle of Fierce Winds Island. "The only other town on the lake with significant extra-human abilities is Hugo on the North shore. The rest—Thunder Point, East End, Larue, Two Lakes probably have a few closet extra-humans and a few Paramortals, but they aren't *out* or in danger of being exposed like here in Destiny."

Dylan went on, "The population is larger here because some of our ancestors who made the blood oath binding all Paramortals stayed here, rather than moving on." There's a reason for that—the fight is here."

CHAPTER 7

Jack

Tues, 11 pm Light years from Mayberry

THE FIGHT WAS *HERE*? Jesus, what fight? What have I gotten my family mixed up in?

"If this is some kind of fight between Paramortals and their enemies why don't they leave the humans out of it?"

He must have seen the look on my face. *TMI* as Jordie would say, but I didn't have a choice. *Negative.* There was always a choice. I could leave this room right now, pick Jordie up from school, grab my parents and get the hell away from Destiny, as far and as fast as I could. But would it do any good?

I recognized the look in Tempe's eyes, imploring, then

shutting down. I saw no judgment there. My stomach felt like it was gnawing its way out of my gut. She would understand if I walked away. I was pretty sure she expected it. Understandable, considering how everyone in her life had exited when the going got rough. I'm sure that's how it felt, whether their intentions were noble or not.

Would leaving this fight be any different than walking away from a battle of human enemies who target innocents, like the terrorists I'd fought in the military? The *Aretuu* didn't sound like they cared who got in their way.

"I take it, these *Aretuu* don't plan to stop at Destiny."

Dylan gave me a nod, *correct*. "They don't discriminate in who they target. Every being on the planet is fair game."

Turning my attention back to Dylan I sighed heavily. "So tell me about this fight." The room seemed to breathe out a sigh of relief as if it were a living entity.

Dylan pulled a chair toward him and straddled it with his arm across the backrest. "The word Paramortal comes from 'para' meaning 'to defend'. It's also a derivative of a word meaning 'more'. That's why the ancestors chose the word to describe those who are more than mortal, who are under blood oath to protect all mankind. It's like a creed. We are under oath, hereditarily and spell bound, to be... good guys, defenders of the defenseless."

Whether he chose those words with intention or not, it hit home. Since the day I went into the service at eighteen that's what I've been, one of the good guys. It's in my DNA.

"Are you starting to feel like one of us yet?" Dylan grinned. He had used those words for a reason: to buffer his next words. "Paramortals come in all shapes and sizes, colors and abilities. Fae, witches, weres like me, Djinn, grey men, you met a Nucklavee, Imps—"

I suppressed a groan. "Next you'll tell me vampires are real."

"—vamps, and the list goes on."

Tempe sat quiet through all of it. I studied her. "What kind of Paramortal are you?"

She stretched her hands out in front of her as if she was just studying her nails. "I'm a Tempestaerie, like my mother. Hopefully." She looked over at Aurora, then back at me, "Or not."

Aurora put her hand on top of Tempe's and squeezed. "Tempe will soon come into her full Tempestaerie power."

My brows lifted as I considered what full power might entail.

Dylan continued, "As I said, children of Paramortals are usually safe away from their parents as long as they haven't come into power. We hoped once River changed, Tempe would follow. That's why I was, uh," he looked at Tempe, "assigned to watch over her."

In an instant, the air got thick and the temperature shot up at least ten degrees. He shrugged unhappily, looked away knowing he'd upset her again.

I asked, "So why didn't that help River, if he's been a true Paramortal since he was fourteen…"

Dylan shook his head. "I can't answer that. They must have tricked him or used his mother or Tempe to get an edge. He'd just gotten his memories back so maybe he wasn't being careful. That's all I can think of."

"So, who's got him? How does this enemy work? And why River?"

Dylan blew out a breath looking over at Aurora. "It's all directed at Dutch. It's why the last nineteen years have been about keeping River and Tempe safe, so they couldn't be used to target Dutch."

I noticed he ignored my other questions. "Good plan," I said sarcastically. "Why Dutch?"

"Dutch is one of the oldest Paramortals in existence, a founder of the Collecte."

Another term I ignored, for now. "How old?"

He watched me closely. "He's at least a few thousand years old—"

"Thousand!" My mouth dropped open.

"But it's not about how old he is. It's about how powerful he is, and how that power could be abused."

"So there are levels of power?" The more I learned, the more everything clicked into place. I felt the rush of excitement as we closed in on an impending resolution to the case—because no matter that it had suddenly taken on an otherworldly big picture, it was still about a murder, a kidnapping, and corruption of power.

Lately, I'd begun to doubt my detective skills but now I knew the reason I'd made no progress—I hadn't had all the facts.

My military training kicked in and delivered a sit-rep. Now I realized what had been a "crime" in the human world was looking more and more like undercover espionage in the Paramortal world, an attempt to take over, by non-human terrorists. This was something I could get my head around after a short self-debriefing.

I rubbed my eyes and got up, stretching my shoulders. It was after eleven and we weren't done. "Aurora, do you have any coffee?"

"Sure," she said and went to the kitchenette to fill the pot.

I leaned against the wall facing Dylan. "Let's say they have River. He's a Djinni. Why do they need Dutch?"

Aurora answered. "Any Djinn is something to be feared. After all, they have the power to grant wishes, and because they can be subjugated under certain circumstances to the wish maker, therein lies the problem. Those who use Djinn are not under The Oath so they can make a Djinni go against his nature. A Djinni would be unable to resist obeying even if it was detrimental to those they love. The older the Djinni, the more *oomph* behind the granted request."

"So…they get more bang for their buck with the head Djinni."

She nodded. "If they were to capture Dutch and request that he annihilate… well, you see the problem."

"Holy—" I let out a long slow breath and looked at Tempe. Her lips did a little upside down quirk that seemed to say, *Bought your tickets yet?*

"What's a Tempest fairy?" I asked her finally.

"Tempes*taerie*," she corrected. "A major Tempestaerie can control the elements, especially air and water, though they will have some influence over fire and earth. Thus—my rain and lightning bolts, such as they were. Minor Tempestaeries like Paige have no significant talent."

"Is that an honest assessment or just two kittens fighting over the milk?" I teased.

"Tempe's understating her potential, Jack," Dylan said. "In the past they've been known to call down asteroids."

That got my attention.

Tempe shrugged and said, "It's not all catastrophic drama though. A storm faerie, as we've been called, can turn into anything associated with weather." She was quiet for a minute then her gaze met mine, and her voice turned soft, sad. "I just remembered—when I was a kid, my first week at school I think, it had been raining for days—the principal's assistant came to my teacher and handed her a pair of black boots. There was a note in them from my mother. It said, "So your little feet will be dry and I can keep my girl close." She turned to me, her eyebrows dipping as tears flooded her eyes. "She'd... turned into a pair of boots, and I walked around with her on my feet all day... long..."

Aurora said, "It was all Phoebe could get away with—"

A few splats of water were the only warning we had before a gentle rain began to fall on every surface of Aurora's workroom. "Oh, dear. It's getting quite unpredictable," Aurora said. I arched a brow at Aurora who looked at Dylan, while she wiped the rain from her skin.

Dylan seemed to be out of patience. He rose advancing on me, staring me down with just a hint of grizzly-face. I rose standing toe to toe while the anger in his eyes sparked. I suspected it was directed mostly at himself. He cared for Tempe and the people here. I respected that. "You in or out, Lang?" he asked abruptly.

I knew my answer but I had a statement to make as well. "Show me your other—what did you call it, your Para —" The air bubbled around Dylan making it hard to discern any of his features, then the dressed in black, dark and deadly man standing eye to eye with me blurred once again into an eight-foot shaggy Sasquatch. His huge paws hung at his sides, level with my shoulders.

I studied *furry-face*, the slavering mouth, the intelligent dark eyes. "Turn around," I ordered.

The creature's head tilted as if to say, *Really?* but he turned as I reached out and tugged on his fur. A sound like a growl escaped and an image from the drive to work the previous week resurfaced. "I saw you, on Grand Pied Boulevard the morning after… damn," I shook my head. "Grand Pied. French, for big foot. How friggin'—"

A bark escaped the massive jaws and the Finrir's eyes glinted with laughter.

I swiped my hands over my face and the air shifted as Dylan turned back, and I was face to face with the man again.

"So, you're in." Dylan's voice sounded deeper, as if his vocal chords hadn't quite made it from growl mode to human. Scratch that, *not human.*

"It's a lot to take in…"

"And no time to play catch up," said Dylan.

Tempe had stiffened, but visibly relaxed when I asked, "Where do we go from here?"

"We find River and take care of whoever is responsible," she said.

"Who do you think killed the Nucklevay?" I asked.

Dylan corrected, "Nucklavee. I'm not sure. Paige and

her partners, Phoebe's protectors, some other entity—human even—though not likely."

"A human, go figure," I muttered. I'd come a long way in two weeks...

Light years.

CHAPTER 8

TEMPE

Wednesday, after midnight Eclipse of the "moons"?

AURORA STOOD UP, fists planted on her hips, a stance I rarely saw from her. "Now that that's settled and we're of *one mind*, we must strategize. The full moon is Thursday night. But most important for River and all Paramortals is the Para-moon, an infrequent coincidence of our moon, Cache´, and the lunar full moon. All Paramortals will gain strength as Cache´ approaches but once the eclipse begins, all power will shut off, like the main switch on a circuit breaker, until the next moon rise."

Jack's eyes narrowed. I could almost feel his cop brain analyzing Aurora's words. "That applies only to Paramortals?"

"Yes. I'm sure you'll have more questions about it but let's take one thing at a time. This increased power will give us some better opportunities to find River. During the full moon, Tempe may be able to renew her mindlink—"

Jack's head swiveled toward mine, his chin sinking as he cocked his head and muttered, "Another of your little talents?"

I shrugged, "Not lately."

Aurora said, "Let's stay focused. During the full moon, whatever force River still has will be stronger, and we may possibly communicate through that mindlink and locate him. If not Thursday, there will be a second chance Friday night, and should we encounter any *Aretuu*, we will be most formidable at that time."

"But powerless after that," Jack said probably thinking of how this would impact the community. "So what's involved and where do we do this mindlink thing?" he asked. He circled his fingers around his right ear, which probably meant he'd decided we were all looney, including himself.

Aurora brought a tray of coffee cups to the table and said, "I think the Forge makes the most sense. There's a strong connection to River and Tempe through their property and it sits as close to the grand pulse as anywhere."

Dylan nodded. "There, or the Big Dead, now that it's no longer dead."

Jack shook his head and I read his expression—*I don't wanna know.*

"The Forge," Dylan said. "Hopefully Jack will come up with a clue after he searches Crain's house. I'll do a little sniffing around the house and his vehicle, and pay another visit to Aladdin's Rub, see if Paige ever showed up for work."

Jack rose. "I need to pick Jordie up. If there isn't anything else I absolutely *must* know, then I'll check with you all in the morning after the search is completed."

I stopped him with a hand on his arm, "Jordie works tomorrow, right?"

He looked down at me, a bit distracted and who wouldn't be with the world as he knew it flipped over onto its axis. "I think so, why?"

"I have a surprise for her. If you're not tied up you might want to be there."

JACK

6:30am His condition was "indeterminate"

I MADE egg white omelets for Jordie and me while I waited for Ryan to call.

"Are you going to pick me up after work tonight?" Jordie asked, taking a bite of her apple. She'd handed me her mid-term grades before going to her room. After she stumbled off to bed I'd remained at the kitchen table trying to figure out where all those brains had come from.

I hadn't been a slouch. *Oh, be honest, Jack. You were a slouch.* But when I found out I needed better grades to do what I wanted to do—get into Officer's Candidate School and become a fighter pilot, only *then* had I cleaned up my act and knuckled down.

Jordie didn't have to knuckle down. She loved school. She loved learning. She also apparently loved being a mentor to other students. Where had that gene come from? Maybe I was selling myself short. After all, I'd excelled in the Navy, climbed the ranks, mentored plenty of younger soldiers.

"I'll be there. Are you going to be able to handle a job and keep up with your homework, in addition to basketball?"

"Sure. The job was one of my goals for this year, to make extra money so that you don't have to pay for everything—"

"Honey—"

"I know, Daddy, but working for Aurora isn't really work. Still, it's time for me to start thinking about taking on responsibility. Before long I'll be graduating."

"Well, in three years," I said, my heart pumping faster just thinking about it.

"Two and a half," she corrected.

And it would be here in a flash, I thought. "So will it embarrass you if I tell you how proud I am of you?" I asked.

"Nope, I can take it." She kissed me on the cheek and went to wash her plate. Turning suddenly, she said, "Oh! I forgot to tell you. Melissa said Mrs. Fortune said that Dr. Shone's vet tech said that Sir Lancelot had to be taken to LSU. He ate a golf club!"

I sighed, and wondered whether to correct her or not. "Mrs. Fortune" is the gossip columnist for the Destiny Tribune. She also works at the Cajun Market in Alliance, and is the local contractor for 1-900-Psychic. I have the sad fate of my daughter being best friends with Melissa Fortune, Jane's daughter, meaning I have to watch everything I tell Jordie. Sometimes, however, I can plant a tidbit I'd like to have circulated through their gossipy teenage network or get a teaser into Jane's column, Fortune's Telling, to reach a particular element or citizen.

"Ms. Fortune said Lancelot's condition was indeterminate." She smiled. "I think she meant undetermined, since it has nothing to do with botany."

Jane Fortune had a penchant for getting her words mixed up and apparently didn't see the importance, even though she was in journalism—if you could call it that—of proofing her work.

"I helped the Game Wardens load him for transport to Baton Rouge. Otherwise, I can't talk about it."

She nodded.

My phone rang. Ryan had picked up Will and was headed to New Orleans. "He says he's hungry so we're going to stop at Cracker Barrel on I-10 and fill him up for the long morning."

"Works for me. Keep him out of the way, and be sure you sit in on the session with the artist," I said.

"Roger that. I'll call you when we leave."

Jordie said, "I've got to run. See you tonight."

I PULLED up to Crain's house thirty minutes later.

The locksmith was on standby but it turned out I didn't need him since the rickety door and the shifting gumbo under the foundation of the house combined to create the perfect walk-in scenario. A gentle push and I was inside. I nodded to my deputy to follow me. "You got the list of what we're looking for?"

Basile nodded. "Yes, sir. That green lid thingie and anything that might link Crain to River or the murder."

"Or Paige Whyte. Look for photos, too, though this guy doesn't look like the sentimental photo-sharing type. He must have been right at home at the Wasted Turtle." I pointed to the trays full of cigarette butts, ashes and burn marks on the furniture and carpet, empty liquor bottles, beer cans, and pizza boxes on the counter between the living room and kitchen. The next time I took a shower the water would probably run gray.

The kitchen sink was almost completely obscured by trash, molded food on plates, and as I got closer the smell rivaled the scene at the clubhouse. With my hands covered in latex I removed food-encrusted pots and dishes to find a half empty carton of curdled milk with a dead mouse floating inside. "Gah, what a slime bucket." But as my eyes traveled the counter above the sink they caught on a cheap chrome whiskey flask, with a mismatched green porcelain stopper. "*Bingo*."

I plucked the stopper from the flask and studied it. There was a crack running from the rubbery edge to the tip and it had been superglued. I guess it worked for a whiskey flask but what about for a genie bottle? "That can't be good."

I dropped the lid into a baggy, zipping it into my jacket pocket. "Basile, I've got the lid, a definite tie to the murder scene and the theft of the amphora. Let's rip this place apart, carefully and thoroughly. If we can find something on paper, an address, a connection to Paige, that might lead us to where River is. The way this guy lives, anything he wrote down, anywhere, could be a clue."

In the end, we found no clues, just more filth. But I counted the search successful because of finding the lid to River's amphora, though we were no closer to finding

River. "Basile, I want you to go home and get your personal vehicle, put on street clothes and stakeout the Wasted Turtle. Keep an eye out for anything suspicious."

"This early?"

"Right now," I confirmed. "And take that folder with you that has the photos in it just in case. I'm headed back to the office to reunite this lid with its bottle."

Tempe

9am Good news, bad news

"I've got the lid," Jack said, as soon as I answered the phone. "To the amphora."

Earlier, he'd left me a text that merely said, "Found plug." I had no idea what he was talking about.

"Oh, good," I said, as I turned into Newcastle subdivision. I'd scheduled a substitute on my route for the rest of the week but Richard, the head clerk, had offered to let me do some package and special deliveries so I could salvage some of my vacation time.

"I expected more enthusiasm," Jack said. "I mean, you went to great lengths to find it, even risked going to jail."

I winced and could have kicked myself. The guy was really trying. He'd called it an *amphora*, instead of a vase. And he knew how important it was to me.

"That's not it, Jack. I'm sorry, I meant to tell you, I arranged for a new one. I was afraid we'd find River and wouldn't have a proper container for his force. It means a lot to me that you called though."

"Well, it's a good news bad news scenario again. The lid is cracked."

"Ah."

"So it's like I figured... wouldn't have been secure enough, right?"

I laughed. "You're really getting the hang of all this magical stuff, Jack."

"Yeah, don't get too excited yet."

"What did you find at Crain's? Anything?"

"No, but finding the lid ties him to the murder scene and River's amphora. I'm going to call Ryan and tell him to bring Crain back as soon as he meets with the sketch artist. No lolly-gagging around for lunch."

"Will's just going to lie to the artist, isn't he?"

Jack said, "You never know. I'll see you this afternoon. You don't want to tell me about Jordie's surprise do you?"

"Nah, what's the fun in that? Please keep me updated, okay?"

"I will."

So, it seemed we were finally getting somewhere. We

knew he and Paige were connected. He'd been at the clubhouse and might've even killed Ray. If we could make the group mindlink work tomorrow night, we could find River. I just wanted this to be over. I wanted River to be safe and well. I wanted a chance to get to know my mother without all the lies between us.

And the biggie that stayed in the back of my mind… I wanted to see my father again. *Zeus' colossal bolts!* I wanted that. Almost as much as I wanted to kill him.

CHAPTER 9

TEMPE

Wed. 3:30 pm 'Serene' isn't a word people associate with me

ON THE JOB stress wasn't nearly as much of a factor in the second week of certifications. I got it now.

My priorities had changed so much in the last ten days that I was no longer worried the big bosses at Universal Mail would let me go over some contrived excuse. I'd been doing my job, and doing it well, for nine years. I had never shirked my duty to my job, but right now, my family was more important.

I could feel the quickening approaching, even stronger since the ceremony Friday night. There was a simmering friction in the cells of my body like vibrating plates on a magician's pole. Any time now they would fly off and go in who knew what direction, cause unknown destruction, because I was unworthy, untrained, and had been... unwilling, but no more.

Jack said Phoebe's house had come back clean as a whistle. After he'd found me there last week, searching for some clue as to where she'd gone, I'd given in and allowed him to have the place processed for fingerprints or—whatever. I hadn't expected him to find anything. I was still hurt that Phoebe and her roomies had moved out and hadn't tried to call me or River, to let us know where they were taking her.

I dropped the last package off and drove back toward town. As soon as I checked in with Richard, I headed downtown to Aurora's. I found a parking spot two blocks away from the shop and grabbed the box out of the bed of my truck. I'd called Jack and told him to meet us early if he could.

When I entered the shop, a tall black woman stood in the center of the mirrored showcase decked out in a purple, green and gold sequined gown. She looked great in the off the shoulder dress but would probably need a fur coat for the frigid weather that was forecast for the weekend.

"Is she the queen or something?" I asked Aurora quietly.

"No, just a member of the Krewe." Another woman exited the dressing rooms, with Jordie holding the long flowing hem of the brilliant white gown. The bodice was covered in glittering stones that reflected light off every surface.

"There's the queen." Aurora turned toward her customer. "Now *that* is you, Selena. I can see why you wanted this style in particular. It's shows off your great figure. Jordie, grab the skirt and swing it around over here so she can step onto the block."

While they worked, I walked to the back room to pour myself a cup of Aurora's special blend. I was pretty sure she put some kind of soothing huju on it, because it always made me feel more serene, and "serene" is not a word most people associate with me. *Oh, you figured that out.*

On one pass through the workroom to get a pair of five-inch high rhinestoned silver heels, Jordie waved hello and returned to the front room. She really was a lovely girl.

Twenty minutes later, the women's purchases were rung up and Aurora asked Jordie to join us in the workroom.

I smiled at Jordie. "We have a surprise for you, young lady. I heard you and your dad are going to be in the Mardi Gras parade next Tuesday, so Aurora and I figured you needed something special to wear. What do you think…?" I removed the bag and revealed a gorgeous pale gold chiffon gown with a rhinestone covered bodice. The skirt fell in the soft rippling colors of the stones decorating the waist.

She gasped and her eyes lit up. "For real? I'm going to

wear that?" She squealed something unintelligible. "Hold it right there. I've got to post this on Instagram and Snapshot. And Pinterest. And People Pages." She took several shots and texted to Cyberland while Aurora and I stood by, waiting for her to try it on.

The world was certainly changing, and I imagined our Paramortal society was already moving in that direction. How long would it be before the otherworldly beings would be tapping into the human social networks to accomplish tasks they'd used magic for? And what of our enemies? Were they already getting up to speed?

"Do I get to try it on?" Jordie asked.

Aurora said, "Well, *ye*ah, when you get through plastering it all over the Internet. Just kidding, Sweetie. First let's do something with that hair."

Aurora had a mini-arsenal of hair products on standby. I hadn't even thought about Jordie's hairdo. Not surprising since I have no sense of fashion. Do the words delivery person and self-contractor impart any clues? My favorite uniform was shorts or jeans and my most indispensable hair item was a box of UMC #10 rubber bands. I was glad Aurora was on the job.

She finished curling the teenager's hair and sweeping it up into an elaborate style. "Now, let's get you into this gown."

Jordie's excitement was obvious as Aurora helped her into some pretty undies and zipped her into the dress. She shook her hands at her sides and jumped back and forth on her toes like an athlete loosening up prior to a game. "Hold still, Missie," said Aurora, as she fluffed and straightened the skirt of the gown. "Okay, now turn around. Slowly!"

We laughed as Jordie twirled in front of the vast expanse of mirrors, looking over her shoulder at the envious faces peering through the window at her, and grinning. I reached into the box and pulled out an intricate hand-made mask of gold, black and red, decorated around the edges with luxurious plumes of red and gold feathers and a detachable gold satin wand.

Jordie squealed, "For me?" She reached out and took it, carefully, fingers trembling.

"It's pretty sturdy," I said. "I wanted something you could enjoy, without thinking about it breaking every time you turn around. Let's see how it looks."

"Wait!" Aurora took the mask from Jordie. "We don't want to mess up all the work I did on that hair or get makeup on the dress." She unhooked one corner of the mask from its elastic string and had me hold it in place while she reattached it. "Now. Let's see what we've got."

Aurora was putting the last touches on Jordie's hair, pulling down curls and straggles when a hiss of breath behind me made me smile. Jack had just gotten a look at his little girl in her first grown-up gown. *Poor Daddy.*

He appeared in the mirror towering over her, blinking several times. I saw what was obvious—pride, tender-ness, fear, and a wealth of love. I'd been drawn to him physically that first day, but it seemed every day that followed revealed yet another surprise into the man's true character.

At first I'd only seen what he wanted me to see—the alpha male in charge, protective father and by-the-rules lawman, but gradually he was letting me in, allowing me glimpses of the vulnerability alongside the strength. It took my breath.

"Sweetheart, I don't think you'll ever be more beautiful than you are right now." He fluttered his hand lightly onto her shoulders. I could tell he needed to hug her but was afraid of messing up the dress, the hair or the mask. He drew back looking at her face, "What's this?" He raised his thumb to her bottom lip, but all three of us cried, "No," as Jordie jerked back out of reach.

"No, Daddy. It's part of the costume. See?" She pooched her bottom lip out. He craned his neck and squinted to look more closely.

Aurora had painted her lips with a satiny gold paint with four little ruby colored dots in the center of her bottom lip. It was made of some kind of waxy goo that would stay in place a few hours unless Jordie accidentally chewed it off. But it would only have to last through Tuesday's parade and then she could change.

Jack said, "Would you do me the honor, My Lady, of allowing me to escort you to your chariot and then to dinner?"

She giggled first then composed herself and said,

"Thank you, kind sir. I would be delighted. But I'll have to change unless we eat out of town, because I can't let anyone see the dress until Tuesday."

"You choose then," said her father.

She turned, "Can Tempe come?"

He only hesitated a second, then identical silver green eyes turned to me, and I nodded. "That would be fun. But I'll need to run home and change."

Jack said, "We'll pick you up. I've got to touch base with Ryan and Peggy. It's 5:05. Is six okay?"

~

Tempe

5:10 pm Was that a lion chasing that Harley?

I'D BEEN BOMBARDED with revelations in the last twenty-four hours that normally would have set me back on my heels. Instead, I found myself with aspirations. The responsibility of raising River had consumed my time, my resources and my focus until he'd graduated from college and his business took off. Then, I'd gotten involved with Dylan.

How exactly had that happened?

It was difficult to remember my time with Dylan and be objective given what I'd learned. Would that new knowledge give me clarity or muddy the waters? I decided to imitate Scarlett O'Hara and think about the relationship later.

One thing was for sure. Without my responsibilities to River hanging over my head, I'd suddenly become aimless, my life without purpose, and feeling very... *hollow. Burned out,* Aurora had said.

So, thinking I needed a project, River and I began remodeling the Voracious Monster. We had a love-hate relationship with our home, Harmony Plantation. I'd felt a lot less harmony after the bills started rolling in, for sure. Especially after replacing the big picture window that over looked the Forge—twice.

Aurora had said working on the house was a way to re-center myself until my "true purpose came to me". *Huh.* I'd forgotten that conversation.

Well, that had changed. Now that I knew Dutch was alive and my mother wasn't guilty of abandoning us, I desperately wanted to see them again. Surely they'd show up soon and help me find River before it was too late.

After my brother was safe, cautious hope whispered, I might feel like I'd found my place in the world I'd been born into. I might even find real love, without lies or games, with someone who would accept me and my little Tempestaerie quirks. I thought of Jack's surprising, if hesitant, support.

We'd made some strides toward finding River. Maybe if

I'd taken the risk and shocked Jack with the truth last week, we'd have found River by now.

As I made the last turn toward home, I caught a flash of silver in my side mirror, near the end of Boggy Bayou Road. Tucking my truck into a vacant driveway next to some hedges, I flipped my lights off and waited. Sure enough, the black and silver Harley roared past, its driver bent low over the bars.

I shivered, suddenly certain the driver of that bike had been following me. Did this have something to do with the disappearances? Was I next? Fear tightened the muscles in my shoulders but then, too late, curiosity took over. Who was behind all this? I should have at least thought to look for the tag number.

The bike disappeared around the curve and I drove down Harmony Lane and into my driveway.

I was surprised to find Katerina waiting for me on the porch. She caught me looking over my shoulder. "What is it, Tempe?" Her dark eyes searched the street behind me.

"Did you see a motorcycle? A big Harley?"

She nodded.

" I think it was following me."

"Let's go inside," Katerina said, and pushed me through the door as I unlocked it, reminding me with the strength of her push that she wasn't human.

"I'll be back," was all she said before she disappeared around the side of the house into the night.

Two minutes later Montana parked behind my truck and strode up the walkway. "Okay, what happened? I saw a puma disappear around the corner of the building and there's no circus in town. So, give."

"I was on my way home and noticed someone following me." Montana was suddenly in Dinnshencha mode. I could tell she was thinking about going after Katerina but her nature being the defender of women, naturally she'd babysit me.

"Have you called the cops?" she asked.

I shook my head, "No. I just got here," I looked at my watch, "and I have to get changed. Jack and Jordie are coming by to pick me up. Jack's the Sheriff, does he count?" She stalked me to the bedroom closet where I flung potential dinner dresses and shoes toward the bed.

"Are you sure this guy was following you?" Montana demanded.

"No. I'm probably making too much of it."

I thought about how the bike had been coming toward my house and... I'd seen it before. I sighed, "Yes."

"Which is it—yes or no?"

"Yes."

"Then we call Jack." She handed me her phone. I rolled my eyes.

"I have a phone," I said sarcastically.

"Then use it," she said.

"I'm going to see him in about fifteen minutes anyway."

"Ah, the dinner you mentioned." She grinned as Kate-rina walked through the front door, looking like she hadn't just turned into a black panther and run wild through the swamp looking for a motorcycle. Black on black, check. Sunglasses, check.

"Nothing?" Montana asked.

Kat shook her head and looked at Tempe. "Where are we going?" She eyed the dress on the bed as I rummaged in the closet for dressier heels. She picked up a pair of pointy-toed black pumps. *Naturally.*

"Dinner with Jack," said Montana. She pointed to the black shoes. "Not those; they're out of style. Throw them out."

"Dinner… as in a date?" asked Kat.

"Not really. Jordie invited me and she's all dressed up. Now if you two want to make yourselves useful, you'll get down here and help me find some shoes that halfway match that dress." I pointed at the knee length navy dress. Montana and Kat exchanged a look. "I'm not going to be dressed nearly good enough to accompany the little Mardi Gras princess and her daddy to dinner as it is. The least I can do is not put them to shame."

"No worries there," said Montana. "You know the eyes

that aren't on that lovely young lady will be on that exquisite hunk of man flesh."

"Wow. Nice compliment. Thanks." I said, wanting to sink between the floorboards.

Kat elbowed Montana. Montana glared. "Ow, Kat. You both know it's true." She smiled at me. "Just accept it. It takes the pressure off you to compete anyway, right?"

I thought about that. "You're absolutely right, Montana. Maybe I'll just wear jeans."

They both jumped in then to help me find something to wear that wouldn't embarrass them as my friends. In the end we chose a silk pantsuit I'd picked up for a song at Twice Around Consignment Shop, which was owned by a friend of ours in Hugo. The design had small teal and black feathers floating across a background of shimmering copper. The material made you want to run your hands over it. I was kinda hoping Jack might feel the urge to do just that.

"Thanks, guys." Just before Montana went out the door, she said, "Don't forget to tell Jack about the motorcycle."

"I won't. I promise."

But I did.

CHAPTER 10

TEMPE

Wed. 7pm Welcome to our parish (now get lost)

JORDIE CHOSE Campbell Green for dinner on the North shore near Hugo, frequented by locals from Hugo and a few tourists. We met a couple from Michigan while waiting on our table who said they had chosen to vacation here because of Storm Lake's *interesting* history, and of course, the scenery.

They held hands as she explained, "We got the brochure from the Louisiana Culture and Tourism Center. We love exploring the weird and unexplainable."

Great. I looked at Jack, who'd pasted his *Welcome to our parish* politician's smile on his face.

She asked about Jordie's dress, if it was a special occasion and *that* led to questions about Mardi Gras and Destiny, when—bless her heart—Jordie mentioned the parade the following Tuesday. I aimed them in the opposite direction of Destiny—Rome, where they could catch a Mardi Gras parade this Friday instead. One local Mardi Gras parade would probably be enough to divert their attention to other attractions and keep them away from our side of ol' Stormy.

There are no signs in Destiny that say *Tourists beware* or *Strangers keep out,* but there aren't any hotels or B&Bs either, except for one, the Faerie Inn.

For Faeries only.

Believe it not, the Fae find our area quite lovely and rejuvenating. Occasionally, a traveler will complain to the Tourism Board about the lack of accommodations, but a complimentary night at Campbell Green or a tour of one of the studios in Larue usually shuts them up.

Campbell Green is an extension of the work that Mystiq Campbell began with the farm and properties she inherited from a relative. She's making quite a name for herself as the caretaker of our environment, at least on the North shore of Storm Lake. Her farm is now mostly green energy or moving in that direction and the restaurant reflected that with natural fresh green displays on each table, CG candles and dishes created at their artisans' barn. It was a warm atmosphere with a scenic view of the water.

Jordie and I had their famous marinated salmon roasted

on a cedar plank. Jack ordered a chargrilled rib eye with all the trimmings. "Good choice, honey," he told Jordie after tasting her salmon.

She smiled. "Melissa's mom said they had the best steak on this end of Storm Lake so I figured you'd like it."

Jack stopped chewing and glanced over his shoulder like he expected the town gossip to pop up at the next table. "Well, she was right."

"It's their special grade of beef, too," I said. "Everything they do is all organic and made or grown at Campbell Green."

Jordie put her napkin down and said, "Can I be excused? I saw one of the girls on the Hugo basketball team in the front room."

When she'd left, I asked, "What happened in New Orleans with the sketch artist?"

Jack put his fork down and sipped his Coke. "After spending a couple hours with Crain, the forensics artist told Kirkwood, Crain was trying very hard *not* to give an accurate composite. At first Will said he couldn't remember, but when our guy pressed him his memory became very accurate. The artist was able to create a second sketch by the features Crain studiously avoided." He reached into his jacket and brought out a copy, placed it in front of me. "Recognize her?"

The woman illustrated in the sketch was clearly Paige.

"Am I biased because I can't stand her, or is that my brother's ex-girlfriend?"

"Nope. It fits her picture ID. Now, we just need to convince him to talk. If he won't, we'll throw him in jail over night. Depending on what happens I'm not sure we can hold him for more than 24 hours."

My shoulders slumped. "Have you heard anything about Lancelot?" I asked.

"The club was the one Mrs. Karrakas ordered. It was confirmed by the manufacturer but that wasn't what made the old alligator sick." He sat back. "He's twenty-three by the way. The vets at LSU gave him an alligator style stomach scope and found a bottle that still retained traces of a powerful drug that would have killed a normal man, and it would have killed Sir Knight if we hadn't found him when we did."

"Is he going to be okay?"

"They think he'll make a full recovery. They're trying to get a read on the drug. That may take a while," Jack said.

"What do you think this means?"

Jack grimaced. "My theory is whoever killed Ray, gave him a dose of that drug and then bashed—used the club to make it look like the murder weapon, possibly to implicate you which would mean our killer isn't very smart; he's very desperate; or, they didn't want Ray identified."

He shook his head. "Every piece in the puzzle means something. We're getting close." He squeezed my hand. "Have faith, okay?"

"I'm trying. I'm just worried we're going to run out of time." I couldn't say the rest, *if we haven't already*, but Jack seemed to read my mind.

"I can feel the noose closing. Hang in there." He tossed his napkin on the table and said, "It's a school night so we'd better collect Jordie and get back to Destiny."

Tempe

10pm Okay, I'll lie, and tell you it's a dog…

WHEN WE GOT to Jack's I was surprised to see Beffie still in residence. He licked my hand and seemed happy to follow Jordie down the hallway to her room, never attempting to jump up on her gown. He behaved better than a real dog!

"How do you like Beffie, Jack?"

Jack looked down the hall then back at me. "Why, did you notice something?"

I shrugged.

"That dog is too good to be true. He almost never needs to go out. He doesn't chew on the furniture or crap in

94

my shoes, and he's devoted to Jordie. If I didn't know better…"

I smiled when I saw him come to a conclusion he couldn't have reached a month ago. "Don't tell me, he's some kind of Paramortal dog? Can't you people leave the animals alone."

I laughed, ignoring the 'you people'. "Okay, I won't tell you, because he's a not a Paramortal. Not every non-human is a Paramortal."

He just shrugged.

"It's a fairy creature whose purpose is protecting households. It often takes the form of a hound, in Beffie's case, a big Catahoula Cur dog, because hey, that's the state dog. You don't like him? I was just thinking he's very well mannered."

"Yeah," he scratched his head, "it just kind of spoils the good feeling of having a canine in the house. I'll get used to it. He looks and acts like a well-trained dog anyway." He cocked his head, eyes narrowed on mine. "Did you arrange that?"

"You mean for Beffie to be here? No, that was Aurora's idea. Jordie was sick and needed a buddy; his previous *job* was done; and he was available. That's all I really know about it—him. It helps when you have to be out late, right?"

"I agree." He looked over his shoulder and gave me the once over. He had that *look* in his eyes, a simmering desire. I felt a matching heat curl in my belly. "Would you like to stay for a cup of Irish coffee. I'll build a fire in the fireplace."

He crowded his body close to mine and took my face in his hands. The kiss was a toe-curler, and I leaned into him. Was he intentionally distracting me from my worries? I smiled liking the plan.

With his arms around my waist he walked me backwards through a doorway and into his office. He eased the door shut behind us guiding me toward the desk with his right arm around my waist. When my butt hit the edge, I leaned against it.

"Jack... Jordie is..." With the moonlight streaming through the windows, his smile was bright.

"Is in bed and we're not doing anything...yet."

I sighed as his hands eased under my top to clasp my waist, one big hand gliding over my skin. "I can't tell where that silky material ends and your skin begins," he whispered into my ear, tonguing the hollow and nipping at my earlobe.

His fingers trailed across my stomach, dipped into my navel. I smiled at the tickling sensation and squirmed. "Ticklish?" he chuckled.

My hands went to his sides, playing over the ridges of muscle. I could feel the heat of his skin through his shirt. I tugged it free of his pants and put my hands on those fine abs. His lips trailed kisses down the side of my face and neck, moved lower as my head *knocked* against the wall and I gasped, "Jack."

A sound of pleasure escaped him as he found my breasts and cupped them. "*Shh.* You'll wake Jordie."

Taking one of my hands, he guided it to the bulge behind his zipper and pressed it there. His tall, wide shouldered silhouette blocked the moonlight when he leaned down to kiss me again. Then his arm tightened around my waist pulling me up to him.

He tasted so good. It felt right being in his arms, kissing him and making love to him. I ached for that to happen. I moaned again and he stopped kissing me, the touch on my breast easing. He placed his hands on my knees spreading them so he could step between, his erection bumping urgently against my pelvic bone.

I reclined against the wall looking up at him, trying to make out his expression. Reaching for my blouse, he unbuttoned the last button, then the next. I felt air hit my skin when he separated the material and leaned over to place kisses on each of my shoulder blades.

His head went lower, his tongue dipping past the rim of my bra, over the tops of my breasts, then, he tugged the cups down, freeing them. I heard his breath just before he put his mouth on my nipple suckling gently while his other hand played with its mate.

I arched up to his mouth. I wanted more. I moaned again and the suckling stopped. He whispered softly, "You aren't going to be a quiet lover are you, sweetheart." His face peered down at me but I couldn't make out his features. "I wouldn't want you to be." He kissed me once more, a deep passionate declaration of what he promised for *later*.

Reluctantly he released my lips, nipping at the bottom one before putting his hand gently over my mouth. He listened briefly, then removed his hand and said quietly, "I guess we'll have to continue this another time." He thrust against me once, took a deep breath, re-situated my bra and proceeded to fasten the buttons on my blouse. I laid my head on his chest, arms wrapped loosely around his waist, smiling, content to feel his heart thumping against my cheek.

"Thank you for what you did for Jordie." He tilted my chin up and looked down into my face. "You and Aurora gave my baby something she's missed; the touch only a woman can give. I know it's important, but I'm out of my depth with the girly things."

"It was a pleasure for us as well, Jack. She was perfection in that outfit wasn't she?"

"Beautiful, but... so grown up. I've only had her with me for a few years now and she's maturing so fast it's scary."

He paused. "She reminded me tonight that she won't be dependent on me much longer. She wants to 'carry her weight'." His sigh was heavy and laden with parental regret as his head touched mine. "I'm not ready for her to grow up, and I don't want her to feel the weight of responsibility on her sixteen year old shoulders.

Dammit. If..." he dropped his hands and stepped back, running his hand through his hair.

"I'm not saying what you went through or did for your brother was wrong, but I hate that you had to carry such a heavy load. It wasn't right. I shouldn't judge though. It sounds like things are different for you—your—people."

I sighed. There it was again. That separation between his world and mine. "I don't know how 'things *are*', Jack. All I know is I was a happy little girl with two parents that loved me and a cute little brother I adored, and suddenly, my family was torn apart, and I had no choice but to grow up and become River's mother and father. It was not an easy task for a young teenager, Paramortal or human, to take over River's care. I don't know about *other* Paramortal families. What I do know is that you are a caring father; Jordie is a happy teenager who knows she's loved and it's her choice to be responsible and contribute, or not. I don't think you have a thing to worry about. She's enjoying school, basketball and her new job. Sounds like you've given her a pretty full life. I think you deserve a pat on the back."

His body shifted so I couldn't see his face. "I'm sorry, Tempe. I didn't mean—"

I leaned across the desk and flipped on the lamp. This was a conversation for the light. "I'm not offended, Jack. I'm finally growing up myself, I guess. I denied my heritage, rejected it." There, I'd said it. I didn't hunch my shoulders or pretend I hadn't meant it, and Jack seemed to really be listening.

"For the first time, I feel like I have a purpose *and* choices. Maybe I always have and just didn't realize it. But before, I didn't know what my options were. I just realized today that I may actually see my family together again." I cleared my throat, and took a slow breath. "It's almost incomprehensible. But nothing is as important right now as saving my brother."

"I want that for you, Tempe. All of it, and I promise to do everything I can to make it happen."

That was saying a lot considering my family never even existed to him before yesterday. For Jack, the last two weeks would have been like going to bed during Top Gun and awakening to Supernatural.

I studied this man who had come so far so fast. "Thank you, Jack. I know you mean it," I said brushing the wrinkles from my shirt. I eased off the desk. "I probably should go. I have to work in the morning—"

"I'm sorry we haven't turned up anything. With nothing concrete to go on, it's a lot of grunt work, driving the streets, passing out flyers and pounding on doors."

"Please promise me you'll call immediately if you hear something."

"I promise," and he sealed it with a deep pulse-pounding kiss.

CHAPTER 11

TEMPE

Thursday, 1pm If it sweats, it's not a toy

BARBARA CALLED, apologizing profusely, but said her daughter had kept her up all night with a stomach virus. She promised she would take over as soon as she got back from the pediatrician's if I still wanted her. I didn't want to be tied down so I told her we'd swap out around lunchtime.

When I arrived at work, the mail center was a nightmare with tubs of junk mail stacked in the aisles and beside mail stations. We're not supposed to call the oversized commercial flyers *junk*, but I am of a mind to call masses of paper ads that end up on the highways, get wadded up and used to light fires and accumulate in mailboxes "trash". *So fire me.*

I piled everything into my truck, yes, even the trash, and took to the street. The morning went very slowly since I had to stop frequently and refill the extra bundle at my side with flyers to be placed alongside each customer's regular mail. I was so used to the physical process that it still gave me too much time to think... and feel guilty, that I was working, and not out searching. The last time I'd talked to Jack that's what it sounded like his deputies were doing.

I passed by the Spanish mission on the way to Enchanted Glen and heard one toll of the bell. The old stone church was no longer in use except on the local tour and for ringing each of the daylight hours. What if he was in there? What if there's a house or an abandoned store, somewhere I pass by everyday and River's there, but *menori* can't sense his presence?

That thought made me want to turn the truck around and beginning at the first house on the block, knock on every door until I'd covered the parish, the entire state if necessary. But I knew that wasn't physically possible. Besides, my customers were aware of River's situation. They'd stepped up big time, distributing flyers, joining the search teams. I'd bet my brother's life he wasn't being held anywhere on my route.

How did I know that River had been kidnapped? I had nothing to go on except my intuition about Paige and the circumstances to say my brother hadn't met some other fate.

The next package requiring a signature was for Mrs.

Trickett, a new customer in a gothic Victorian that would have fit right in down in New Orleans. It was a narrow purple two story with gold trim and Mardi Gras beads strung along the ornately designed porch railing. I got the feeling this was a year round design statement, not just for the upcoming holiday.

A slender giant of a man answered the door and asked me in. "Please make yourself at home. I'll be right back. I need to turn the fire off on the stove and wash my hands." Even in the high ceilinged rooms it was necessary for him to duck to get through the doorway.

He left me in a cozy living room of French provincial furniture mingled with child-sized duplicates, including a plushly upholstered high chair. If not for those high ceilings, I would have found the tiny rooms claustrophobic. A life-like doll was propped on the fireplace mantel, her neck wrapped with Mardi Gras beads that swung down over the stone, casting firelight around the room like cheap diamonds.

She was a little *too* life-like, the moisture trickling down the *doll's* temples a dead giveaway. I respected her right to be incognito so I didn't stare, but I couldn't help but think if she was a faerie and the tall guy was her son… "That had to be painful."

"You have no idea."

I jerked. The little faerie's rigid posture relaxed and she wiped the sweat from her skin, moving butt over hands to the end of the mantel, careful not to catch the fabric of her skirt. The young man returned and ran to her side, glancing at me, ready to take on any threat to his mother. "Mom, be careful."

"Sit down, Junior," she said and gathering the crisp taffeta in two fists, leapt from the mantel to make a perfect landing in the elaborately decorated high chair. "I haven't lived all these years without adapting to my lack of height. Sign for the package will you, Val?" she smiled at her son. Then she turned to me. "You're Tempest Pomeroy, aren't you?"

I gaped. How did this little faerie know me? I'd never delivered her mail before today. While I scanned the package and held the form for her son to sign, she explained, "I'm friends with Phoebe and Dutch. We go way back."

How far back, I wondered. She smiled, anticipating me. "Since before you were born. But, that story will have to wait for another time. You have work to do and a lead to follow."

I stared at her. *What lead?* The subject of her past was apparently closed... for now.

Val still hovered over his mother and she waved her hand at him, "Val's friends think I died in childbirth. So on the rare occasion that he brings a girlfriend home, I must play the *stuk speelgoed*—I'm sorry, my mum's word— a child's toy."

Val sighed, "She's forever being picked up and tossed around like a play thing." His shoulders slumped. It was obvious he loved his mother very much. "Luckily she heals quickly." His eyes glinted. "I have to stay close in case the *doll* bleeds or sweats. That's when she's in danger of being exposed."

"If you wouldn't keep the house fire so high, son..." When Val returned to the kitchen, she said, "He's very protective. But enough about us, have you found your brother yet?"

"How..."

Mrs. Trickett rolled her eyes and dropped her head back on her chair. "Novices. Girl, you need to spend more time with Aurora like your parents intended. Then you'd know what's going on around here. Tell me this. Are you aware that a fae guest went missing from Bella and Petre's Inn?"

Bella and Petre ran the only B&B in Destiny, the Faerie Inn. If a fae had gone missing recently it might have something to do with River's disappearance.

Arabella and I usually had coffee together by the swamp on weekends but since River had disappeared, I hadn't seen her.

"No, I wasn't aware of that, Mrs. Trickett," my embarrassment was replaced by curiosity.

"You need to talk to them asap," she said, firmly. "Then when this all blows over, come back and we'll talk about the old times. Bring your mother."

Bring my mother. Last week that comment might have

received a "Not on *Zeus' immortal life!*" but things were different now. I was different now. I'd learned almost as much about Destiny as Jack had.

"I'd like that, Mrs. Trickett." She'd leaned forward, waving me down for a hug. Awkwardly, I bent over and pressed my cheek to her lips, accepting the kiss and a motherly pat on my elbow, which was as far as she could reach. "Thanks for the lead," I said. I let myself out and jogged out to my truck, dialing my sub as I cranked the engine. By now you know how much trouble I'd be in if I left the route holding all the mail. But if Barbara couldn't meet me en route, it couldn't be helped. I was going to make a detour to the Faerie Inn.

CHAPTER 12

As luck would have it—Barbara's not mine, because I hadn't been terribly lucky lately—she turned the corner as I drove away from the Tricketts'. I apologized to Barbara for just tossing all the mail into her truck and racing off, but it was imperative that I check out the faerie's lead.

She'd called me a novice. Well, she was right, but I was quickly getting up to speed on all things Paramortal.

I called Jack to find out what he'd been able to get out of Crain. "You might want to ask Will about a missing faerie. Can you handle that?"

There was a pause on his end of the line. "I'm… not sure I'm capable of asking that question of a human in an investigation with a straight face but I guess if I have to, I can go to the men's restroom and practice in the mirror," he answered sarcastically. "I'm turning into a character in a fantasy, Lord Sheriff of the 'Rings'." He changed the subject. "Are you still on the mail route?"

"No. My last customer gave me a tip. One of the Fae has gone missing recently. I'm headed over to the Faerie Inn. I'll talk to my friend, Bella, and see if there's anything to it and how it relates to River."

I didn't volunteer any information about Petre and Arabella. *That* he would have to see for himself. Any other time I might have been entertained by his intro-duction into Bella's world at the Faerie Inn.

Arabella's home is a grand antebellum-style two-story mansion. Elaborate gardens wind along the circle drive, and around both sides of the house to a large pond shaded by hundred and fifty-year-old live oaks. Wall to wall French doors line the front of the house.

Driving through the black gate between the wide peach colored columns on either side of the circle drive, most people are struck speechless by the sight of the grand double staircase shaped like the graceful outward-bending necks of two swans. The balustrade is white, the steps a shiny black as the curving *necks* wind toward the second floor.

Dead center between the stairs spanning both floors is one giant set of forty-foot doors, making this mansion a little less antebellum and a bit more *Arabellam*. It's designed to accommodate all shapes and sizes of faeries, but especially Petre.

The nearest B&B to this Inn is the one at Campbell

Green but it's actually meant for tourists. This inn is always reported as over booked, but the place is so awe-inspiring that occasionally tourists drive up and beg to be placed on the Inn's long (non-existent) waiting list. If they actually made it inside they wouldn't get to see the same place as I due to some creative glamour.

My feet hit the front walkway and the tall golden doors slid open without a sound, my friend Arabella gliding out, as graceful and elegant as her home. If she hadn't been a faerie queen, she would have made a great fashion model.

"Tempest, how lovely to see you. I missed our morning tea this week." She brushed a kiss against my cheek.

"I did too, Bella."

Most weekends when I'm off, Bella flies over to Harmony to sip tea and enjoy the rejuvenating effects of the Forge with me. Or hunt for her breakfast.

She studied my face, finding something there to make her squeeze me in a hug. "You're just in time to share a meal. Actually, we were getting the hog and trimmings ready for supper but since you're here, we'll just serve it for lunch. Come in."

I didn't bother to argue but followed her inside. I loved this place. Upon entering, one left the earthly plane of Destiny and entered the abundant botanical world of the Fae. Even the interior was like an outdoor entertainment area with a trickling spring dumping into a pool of blue surrounded by lush flora. Tiny creatures lounged on flat rocks and lily pads and frolicked in the water.

In the kitchen, an ancient looking stone hearth with open black iron doors provided a view straight through to the luxuriant forest out back.

"It's been too long, Tempest," a voice echoed as if it came from the deepest well. I turned. Petre, Arabella's mate and the Fae king, unfolded his long, sylph-like body from his seat near the little brook and leaned against the stone wall. His slender green hand patted me gently on the shoulder. I came up to about thigh-high on Petre.

"Hello, Your Highness." I tipped my head forward.

"Now, now, none of that."

Arabella said, "Relax for a bit while I put the pig in the oven." Bending over, the beautiful but frail-looking faerie lifted a wide iron roaster with a stuffed boar hog in it and turned toward the massive black hearth.

Petre said, "Darling, I'll get that for you." He bent to pluck the two iron doors off the front of the oven so Bella could place the big boar onto the floor of the wide oven.

Just before he replaced the heavy doors I got a glimpse of some of the faeries in the backyard. Returning to the lounging room, he collapsed to the floor in a lotus position and held out his hand to Bella, who stepped onto one knee and climbed into position on his shoulder, one leg crossed elegantly over the other.

"Tell us why you've come. Does it have something to do with River?" asked Petre.

I shrugged, grateful for their consideration and attentiveness. "I can't believe I haven't been out here to talk to you since all of this began. You know so much and always have your antennae up. It seems like all I hear is 'why didn't I know any of this was happening' or 'if I'd only been studying the path I'd have been'..." My complaining petered out.

Bella sighed and leaned back against Petre's wide torso while he stroked her pale skin. "It's so easy for others to blame or use hindsight to criticize once something's happened, but that's not our way, Tempest. You traveled the path you were mean to travel. No matter where you are, or what's happened to concern or delight, it is the path. Don't take on others' recriminations. They will just get in the way of your progress today."

I sighed. "You sound like Aurora. She just gave me that identical speech," and it was sounding less like it came off a tarot card each time I heard it. "She said I needed to learn to live my *truth.*"

Bella smiled and tipped her head in agreement. "Which is why so many of us turn to Aurora for counsel." That made my brows wing up. The heads of the Fae realm turning to Aurora for advice? I'd have to remember to ask her about that.

"I just met a lady on my route, a Mrs. Trickett, and she said one of your guests had gone missing. Is that true?"

Petre nodded. "Partially true, yes. Sariel, a fae from Fierce Winds Isle, was due here last week but never arrived. We haven't determined if there was... what's the term..."

"Foul play?" I offered.

He tipped his head. "That has not been determined."

Arabella rose and slid from Petre's lap. "Come outside, dinner is almost ready."

Almost ready? She'd just put the pig in the oven. She led me out of the kitchen to where the yard became a field of flowers, dogwoods and cherry blossoms. Bella looped a basket over my arm and pointed at various herbs and blossoms. I followed her example dropping the ones I picked into my basket.

Before long we were back at the house, and I realized I was looking into the house through the large oven once again. Bella tossed the herbs and blossoms into the oven and had me do the same. Then she called to Petre, "Honey, would you please get the pig out before it overcooks." She winked at me.

The giant fae king appeared at Bella's side, easing the sizzling tray one handed onto the large table. I had watched the tray with the uncooked boar enter the hearth less than ten minutes before, but the pig Petre removed was redolent of spices, stuffed with fruit, the blossoms forming a flurry of glazed flower shaped imprints on the succulent brown skin. How did I forget, that for faeries like Petre and Bella, an oven wasn't really necessary, merely… ambience.

"Stay for lunch?"

I hadn't forgotten I'd come on a mission. "I thank you," I said formally, "but I need to know if you think this faerie's disappearance had anything to do with River's."

Petre said, "That probably depends on what the investigator finds."

"So, who's in charge of finding out?" I looked at Bella whose thoughts had strayed to the table preparations.

"Finding out—oh, about the foul play?" Bella cocked her head and frowned at me, "Why, Dylan, of course."

I threw up my hands. "*Zeus' lacy drawers!*" Once again, something I should have known. Or you'd think I would have figured it out. Maybe if everyone hadn't been so determined to keep so many secrets from me, I would have.

I looked at Bella, my voice rising, "How many times have we sat by the bayou, visiting?" My voice rose and *menori* came alive inside me, like an irritated cat, whipping me with her tail. I could hear myself chastising my friends but couldn't seem to stop. "Was there ever a time you thought about telling me the 'way of things' or that Dutch was alive? That Dylan was doing undercover faerie investigations?"

I felt the aura of the powerful presence first, like a big blip on my radar. The smaller faeries dove under bushes and went running for the forest. Then a voice boomed, reverberating off the stone wall of the house, thundering through the trees.

"Tempest. Stop."

Tempe

She's come undone... a Tempestaerie fugue.

I RECOGNIZED HIM... by the voice that had been likened to bellowing organs, crying out rain over the mountains to flood rivers, sending fire to create fear and move rock.

Menori recognized the familial wind. She skyrocketed through my system, flushed blood through my arteries. Impulses of neurotransmissions crashed and exploded like missiles in a giant conductor making the tendrils of her bonds loosen and stretch, preparing to strike.

If not for that... the man might have been a stranger. Tall, massively built, bronze from head to black leather biker boots—think Dwayne 'The Rock' Johnson on mega steroids, and that's *before* he goes full-on freaky Djinn. This *man* had a heavy mane of burnished copper hair streaked with color. The father I remembered had been bald, but the last time I'd seen him, I'd been seven years old. *And* I'd been told he was dead.

My chest was being clawed apart from the inside, pulsing to the beat of my anguished heart. Any second it would blow out like a deep sea oil well, leaving havoc in its wake.

"Dutch." *Menori's* control made my voice calm.

"Tempest."

Wait, motorcycle boots, black leather... "You! The rider who followed me, who staked out my house, watched me come and go, but didn't have the parental consideration, or love, or decency to knock on my door and reintroduce yourself... say, 'oh, sorry honey—you grieved for nothing, belittled your mother undeservedly and because of me, your little brother may d-die!' How about that, Father?" I choked.

And couldn't stop it.

He crossed his arms and gritted his teeth the second I unleashed the fury of my wrath at him.

On the periphery of my vision, I saw a protective shield rise like a dome over the picnic table and faerie guests who stood against the transparent barrier, gaping and pointing at the out of control weather berzerker. I glared at them, my eyes lit with a hot inner sunlight. They scampered away diving under the table.

"It's me you're angry with, daughter. Unleash your fury here!" He pounded his enormous chest and flexed hulking arms of bronze. As if those were the magic words, I came... *unglued.*

Wind roared and slammed into him, but his body was like a mountain—immovable. Rain pounded in big fat drops, and baseball sized hail fell on the backyard until he was standing in a foot of it, and still he stood, like a granite monolith. Shards of ice bounced off his impenetrable skin.

I called lightning, big honking bolts of jagged blue that ripped across the sky and slammed into the ground at his feet. And closer. He deflected those, and smiled.

I raged. What could bring down a mountain—a flood, but he was not made of dirt. Frustrated I gathered *menori* around me and jacking up the speed of my spin, directed all of the rocks around the pond into *menori's* new power...

Someone shouted. "No. Tempest."

Before the small boulders went ten feet, he rose making use of the pond to become a giant waterspout. I dropped the rocks, gathered the forces of air and heat and aimed a straight-line wind at the center of the whirlwind. I'd break through that vortex and he'd have to regroup—

"Tempe, my God, stop."

My Tempestaerie rejected the human voice off hand. She was angry. *Danger.*

I turned, and she aimed at...*him*. Jack.

Then I was knocked to the ground by one of my own

CRY ME A RIVER

missiles, or my father directed it at me to make me snap out of the Tempestaerie fugue. It worked.

When I opened my eyes, Jack was bending over me. Over his shoulder, I saw the spout collapse, slide down over itself and blink out. Then Dutch was there as well. Jack turned his head and looked at Dutch, as if he saw men turn into waterspouts and women throwing boulders and—I looked past them to Petre—and twenty-foot tall green men standing by laughing at the whole scene, everyday.

He said, "Dutch Pomeroy, I presume." It was so bizarre I almost laughed.

Jack

After-freakin' noon

Imagine meeting an alien in person

I COULD SAY that Tempe's father was... not what I'd expected. That would be like saying I could imagine meeting an extraterrestrial-being face to face.

In his human *form*—scratch that—if he'd been *human*, he would be the biggest, most imposing man I'd ever seen. Except for the fact that he was all bronze and had thick bushy red hair sporting the same bright streaks as Tempe's, he could have been the Hulk. Now I knew why the motorcycle parked on the driveway looked like the 4XL model.

Hearing the distant storm and suspecting it meant Tempe was in action, I'd taken off around the side of the house but the scene in the backyard of the stately mansion left me momentarily speechless.

Full beast mode was my first thought as I watched Tempe's burgeoning power billow out in all its glory. I couldn't take my eyes off of her. She was taller, more… just… more, her colorful mane replaced by undulating… images? An illusion? It couldn't be real… huge crashing waves, as if all the disasters at sea over the centuries were being played out fresh in her rainbow tresses.

I saw a ship sinking, another plummeting from atop a mighty foaming peak, and what looked like Poseidon leading a chariot of watery steeds through the waves. The churning waves extended down her arms and lightning flickered along her limbs and between her breasts.

Wind whirled around her like the churning vortex of a tornado but only the things she directed with her eyes and her hand became ammunition.

Dutch seemed to be operating purely on defense, allowing Tempe to throw everything at him without responding. At first the corded muscles in his legs had seemed to… plant themselves… like roots into the ground.

But then the lower half of his body became indistinct

like the figure on River's old amphora. A genie-in-a-bottle cartoon from an ancient commercial came to mind suddenly, and that image would be worth a chuckle... later, if I lived through this version.

I turned my attention back to the Tempest, for she certainly deserved that name as she hurled an entire world of meteorological forces at Dutch, with no effect. That is, no effect on him. Her efforts were laying waste to the outside of the house and the expensively land-scaped property, not to mention endangering the people in the backyard who had been getting ready for a cook-out. Her frustration was evident and I feared she hadn't reached the peak of her power yet. Then I remembered what Dylan said, that *Tempestaeries had been known to call down asteroids...*

Something moved near the house, some kind of thick green vines. I tilted my head back to see a tall rather handsome *green* giant looking down and smiling benefi-cently at me. I faltered at the sight but a rock the size of my head flew by narrowly missing me, and I was pulled back to the fight between the two Pomeroys.

While my attention had been diverted, Dutch's Hulk sized body had become a waterspout spinning up water from the pond a hundred feet into the air. And Tempe was now a full-blown tornado, directing rocks, garden tools, anything but us spectators, with just her gaze. She no longer looked human. Her irises were like looking down the swirling eye of an F-5 tornado. And if that was what she was going to do with the debris in her control, she had to be stopped.

I slugged my way, one wind ravaged step at a time, partially covering my face and eyes to protect them from the flying detritus, and forced myself between the father and my storm-mad virago.

CHAPTER 13

TEMPE

You haven't seen nuclear

JACK'S concerned face looked down at me. Above him was clear blue sky, clearer than it had been twenty minutes ago since *menori* and I had sucked nearly all the moisture out of the atmosphere.

One second I'd been watching Petre take the pig from the oven and the next... "What happened?" I asked, as more faces peered down at me, blocking the sky from my view. I shut my eyes and my head thunked against the ground. "I finally lost it, didn't I?"

"Yep—" Jack.

"Finally—" Dutch.

My eyes popped open and I went from relaxed to ignition in a flash.

Jack raised his hands. "Hey, how about we try some verbal crisis management for a change? It didn't look like the indiscriminate missile launching was getting either of you anywhere. Not towards finding River at any rate."

That got through because he was right.

My father's massive paw appeared in front of me and I took it. I wasn't sure where all that anger came from. He tugged me onto my feet and into his arms, his hold vise-like in the brief seconds it took for me to give in to my eternal longing for him. I let loose the pent up grief, turmoil and relief, and absorbed the tender devotion I felt fully through the Qi'mele, the core of our Paramortal power.

Devotion. The certainty of my parents' and other Paramortals' dedication to mine, and River's well being, hit like the force of a microburst. Our safety and longevity had to be assured before they could worry about our happiness—or our feelings. Tension drained out of me as I looked up at him. He wiped my tears away with his thumbs and waited.

Except for the shoulder length streaked hair (so that's where it came from)... "You look the same."

As first lines following a big fight and a nineteen-year separation went, it wasn't much, but I was trying for normalcy. There I went again, holding up my world to someone else's standards. My idea of normalcy ran completely counter to Jack's. I glanced at him.

Jack Lang was a complete anomaly. After placing so much emphasis on his unrealistic expectations of Destiny, he'd landed unexpectedly and with some degree of comfort on the opposite side of the normal. Either he was on his way to accepting the way things were, or he was in a shock induced coma.

While dear old 'dad' and I embraced, Jack took in the scene around him. No one was making any pains to hide their nature, so I watched him while Arabella and Petre magically righted the table and returned the roasted pig to its pre-storm state; while Neil, the resident ogre picked up the debris I'd flung about; and a myriad of other fantastical creatures scampered around as if he were invisible. He seemed to be taking it in stride. He hadn't so much as blinked. I decided he was in shock.

"Jack, are you okay?"

He faced me, eyes going from wide-eyed wonder to slant-eyed consideration. He directed that look at Dutch. "Was it necessary to let her go nearly nuclear?"

Dutch's eyebrow disappeared into his hair. He wasn't questioned—ever. "It was, yes." His voice sounded as if it was set on *megaphone low*. "And you haven't seen nuclear. I've heard good things about you, Lang, you should be glad of it."

It was Jack's turn to hike the brow. As human threats went it wasn't much, but coming from Dutch it was the only notice you'd get before you were annihilated. I put a hand on Jack's arm, causing Dutch's eyes to widen, then sharpen. *So it's like that, is it, daughter?*

I gasped, and Jack nearly went for his gun. I grabbed his arm. "It's okay, Jack." I scrunched my eyes shut and thought as hard as I could in my father's direction, *Is that what a mindlink sounds like?* It had been so long.

Dutch's chest rumbled with laughter. "There's no need to shout or make faces, Tempest. Simply open your mind to me and speak through it."

Jack nodded, as if verifying some assumption. "I hate to break up this little reunion," he said, "but we have work to do if we're going to try this telepathy thing to find River." He held our gazes as he reached into his pocket. "We searched Crain's yesterday and found this." He held out the back door of River's original amphora to Dutch.

Dutch plucked it from Jack's hand. "It's cracked! He can't use an amphora with a damaged door," he said, in a voice one decibel beneath a roar.

I took the lid from Jack's hand. "Good thinking, Jack. The old amphora will make an excellent focal point for the gathering tonight, now that I have the *replacement* amphora ready." I gave Dutch a pointed look.

A Djinn of Dutch's stature didn't know the meaning of 'contrite' so he settled for, "Hmm."

Jack moved on. "I have some ideas about that. But we have things to do before we head to the swamp.

Everyone will be gathering there to lend their, er, do whatever you do at these things."

Dutch perked up, "What swamp? Big Morte?"

I said, "Big Morte is no more, Dutch. We're going to try to get through to River tonight at the Forge, during full moon."

Dutch went still. "This was Aurora's idea?"

A frisson of unease passed over me. "Aurora's and Dylan's, why?"

He shrugged. "Let's go."

"What is it?" I pressed.

He placed both of his large hands on my shoulders and his eyes went meaningfully to Jack's behind me. "It's… late, daughter, and I'm not sure your brother will have enough *Qi'mele* to transmit outside his body."

I swallowed. "You mean we might be too late."

"Don't give up yet, Tempest. They don't call me the most powerful Djinn for nothing." But the worried look he cast over my shoulder belied those words.

*J*ACK

I LOOKED AT MY WATCH. A little less than three hours before we were due at Lightning Bayou, or the Forge as the Paramortals called it. My cell vibrated. "Yeah, Ryan."

"Jack, Crain wouldn't give Paige up. He stuck to that story about her setting him up, planting the 'green stopper'. He lawyered up and we had to let him go. He *said* he had to go to work, but I checked. He didn't show. Thought you'd want to know he's on the way home, or more likely... he's in the wind."

"That's a stroke of bad luck," I said as Dutch's eyes narrowed. "Basile's at the Wasted Turtle. Peggy is searching the records down at the courthouse to see if there's anything that can help us locate them. Keep hitting those back roads and monitoring the scanner." I looked at Tempe and Dutch. "Our luck is going to turn. I just know it."

A genie eye roll followed that statement. Someone's cell phone went off and we all looked around. A slender young boy stooped to pick up a piece of debris and with his purple tinted hand reached toward Tempe. She thanked him and took the phone. Her cell phone brand should be worth a fortune, if a storm like hers couldn't kill it.

"What is it, Dylan?" Her frustration was evident. Time was not on River's side. She listened for a couple minutes shaking her head. Ending the call she looked at me then Dutch. "He was calling from Aladdin's Rub." She clarified for Dutch, "That's where Paige, the woman we think took River, works as a housekeeper." She looked back at me. "He was going to *influence* the manager to give him Paige's address. The manager heard about the trouble she's in and she hasn't shown up to work since Sunday, so he gladly gave Dylan the information. Unfortunately, her place is empty. Dylan said no sign of her being there in days."

She sighed, her shoulders dropping. She looked frazzled which one would expect after becoming a wind driven mini-hurricane. I yearned to put my arm around her and give her a hug, but her giant copper papa was giving me *the eye* and I couldn't quite bring myself to test him.

Maybe another time.

CHAPTER 14

Tempe

"Here, hold that tree."

FRED CALLED—ONCE again at a most inconvenient time —to tell me he'd decided to take down the tree next to the house, which had been damaged over the winter, even though we'd discussed it and I'd told him to wait until River could be there.

Then he dropped the second little bomb, "I found a text from River from last Sunday night. I'm sorry, Tempe, I must have missed it."

"I'll be there as soon as I can, Freddie. Don't cut that tree until I get there," I said, but had a feeling he couldn't hear me over the sound of the chain saw. It was highly likely that Freddie, our unhandy handyman was about to destroy my new roof and take out the picture window for the third time. I called Jack and told him about the text and where I was headed. He said he'd meet me.

I drove up in the yard beside Harmony. The chain saw was running but Freddie wasn't holding it. He was looping a rope around the thick sixty-foot tall pine. I assessed the situation quickly and saw several problems. The chainsaw sat wobbling near Freddie's foot. He'd made a sizable cut in the base of the tree, on the wrong side, and the breeze was making it sway in the direction of the house. I ran to him, leaning over to hit the kill switch on the chain saw first. As I rose, Freddie shoved the rope into my hands and said, "Here, hold that tree."

I took the rope automatically, wondering what in the hell he was thinking. Scratch that. He wasn't thinking. He's *Toolman*.

I looked up, and up, at the old pine which was swaying a bit more in the wrong direction. A woman my size wasn't about to keep a tree this big from toppling like it was fixin' to. Strong hands gripped mine and I looked over to see Jack, the corded muscles in his arms straining as the tree started to fall inexorably toward the house.

"Can't you do something?" Jack asked quickly, his boots starting to skid on the grass and loose dirt.

"Do something?" I put every one of my hundred and twenty pounds into pulling with him. Freddie had pulled the truck around and was backing up to us.

Jack said, "Fred, hurry. Wind that end around the trailer hitch." But it wasn't going to happen fast enough. "Tempe, how about using that wind power of yours to right this tree where we can send it in the other direction *before* it destroys your house."

Why didn't I think of that? Because every time I tried to use my powers on purpose it didn't turn out like I imagined or planned? I closed my eyes, called *menori* and gathered the wind. It came... easily, surprising me with its obedience? It felt alive, responsive, and I reveled in the tactile sensation of collaboration and control.

"Tempe... what are you waiting for?" Jack's voice was strained.

"Oh, right." It took no eye scrunching, grunting or wishing. My inherited wind, *menori*, simply embraced the trunk and eased it in the opposite direction, until Jack realized what was happening and let go of the rope. He looked over his shoulder and pointed toward a vacant spot between my house and the neighbors. I *aimed*—that's the only way I can describe it—the tree in that direction. We heard a crack when the saw-cut widened across the trunk and Jack pulled Freddie out of the path of the tree as it toppled to the ground.

Jack brushed his hands off. "Unorthodox, but effective, Storm Lady." Jack gave me an enthusiastic kiss then turned to Freddie. "Fred, Ms. Tempe says you got a text from River. Can I see it?"

Freddie looked at me and I nodded. He pulled the

phone out of his pocket and scrolled down. It had been sent on the Sunday evening River disappeared.

F. have to meet an old girlfriend, about a friend of my mother's. Will give you a list of projects when I see you tomorrow or the next day.

"Is this the only one, Fred?"

"Yes, sir. I'm sorry I didn't see it until today, Tempe."

"It's all right, Freddie, why don't you clean things up, or if you want to, start cutting the trunk. But when we leave, you need to go home as well. From now on, when I say wait, you wait until either River or I can supervise."

"Yes, Ms. Tempe," his shoulders slumping as he nodded and turned away.

I shook my head. "I haven't been making my instructions to Freddie clear enough."

Jack said, "That's the thing about confidence, sweetheart. What you gain in one area of your life naturally spreads to others. It'll work out. At least Freddie's heart is in the right place. You have to admire his work ethic." He grinned.

"Do you think it would have made a difference if we'd seen that text *last* week?" I asked.

"You never know, Tempe. We were going in that general direction anyway thanks to your instincts about Paige."

"River mentioned one of mother's 'friends'. I wonder what River was thinking."

"We'll ask Paige and River when we find them. Come on. You have an appointment to keep and I need to check in with Jordie."

~

Tempe

Thur 5:53pm A full Tempest moon in the house of family

"WHEN ARE you going to sign me up for the derby?"

I turned. We'd gathered at the eastern most edge of Lightning Bayou behind Harmony with about fifteen of our closest friends and family. The troublesome Imp— yes, that's redundant but it bears repeating when it comes to Marty—had just spoken to me and he was nowhere in sight.

"Marty…" I hissed, "where are you?"

Aurora explained quietly to Jack, "The name, Forge, comes from *Lei Vis* meaning light force, given not to this shallow marsh that runs throughout Destiny, but to the super pulse of leylines that lies beneath it. For Paramortals it's akin to the most elite health spa for restoring and re-energizing one's *Qi*."

Jack scratched his head. You had to give him credit for trying to soak up everything. I wasn't sure how much more he could take in. Then Aurora continued about how the full moon this month was in a good position for our mindlink since it was in the fourth house of family opposite the tenth for the mother's influence.

Jack said, "I don't believe in Astrology." He paused, probably realizing he hadn't believed in fairies either until last week. "So when will the moons be colliding?" he asked Aurora.

Aurora smiled, "Clever, Jack. It's called coinciding and it's not as predictable as with the celestial moons. But to answer your question right now I estimate the coincidence between Sunday and Tuesday."

Dutch arrived and Aurora embraced him, but Dylan merely nodded. *What was that about?*

"*I know what it was about,*" Marty's voice came again and this time I heard it in my head.

The mindlink? I stared at the ground where the sound had come from. "Marty, where *are* you?" Milling around and keeping their voices low as Aurora had instructed, were Montana, Kat, Bailey, even Arabella, though Petre had remained at the Inn. I did not see the Imp.

"I'm sitting in front of you," he said. "I'm invisible."

Duh. "You can do that?"

"Careful, lass, you'll look crazy if you keep talking to the ground."

"How… and why are you invisible? We could use you

here at the circle."

His voice came, low and sincere, "That's why I'm here, Tempest. But I'd rather stay under the radar with humans about, and it doesn't make sense you'd bring any of your dogs, now does it?"

I was struck simultaneously with relief and irritation. "Thank you, Marty. But... what do you really want?"

"I'm here to boost the chances of connecting with River, though I must tell you I've been trying for days and I've detected nothing. And he—" Marty hushed as Jack, Aurora and Dutch approached from opposite ends of the yard. I'd been distracted and hadn't noticed.

A car door slammed. Andy and Jordie appeared at the top of the slope carrying on an animated conversation, which stopped abruptly when they saw Jack's glare. "What are they here for?" he asked Aurora. "I thought only POPs were invited." He looked like he might grab his daughter and leave.

"What's a POP?" Dutch grunted, frowning at Jack. He must have been using glamour because he looked less like a copper giant, but still acted like a big noisy kid in a quiet church meeting.

"I'll tell you later," I whispered.

Aurora's eyes met Jack's. Time seemed to slow. Jack's sternly frowning face turned neutral. He relaxed and nodded. "I... you invited Jordie?"

"Yes, Jack, we make exceptions. She wanted to come, so

with your permission I'll allow it. She's in no danger. Think of the ritual as a seanc—a prayer circle."

Jack put his arm around Jordie and squeezed. Jordie looked at her father expectantly. He sighed, cast a glance at me and nodded. I'd sensed something from Aurora for a second. Had she put some kind of hoodoo on Jack?

Apparently it was one thing for him to be in the vicinity of *you people* but quite another for his daughter. I was having a hard time coming up with any animosity toward him though. If I'd been in his shoes the last two weeks, I probably would have packed up my daughter and moved in the dead of night. They'd both grown on me, and I didn't want anything to happen to either of them.

I wondered how much Jordie knew. She'd found out about the event somehow, maybe from Andy, and begged Aurora to come. Aurora had told her it was like channeling, saying there was a strong 'family bond' between me, River and Dutch that we were hoping to use to find River. That was actually pretty close.

"Quiet everyone." Aurora's authoritative whisper traveled across the yard. "Dylan, break out the ritual supplies. We must be in place by 6:53 and maintain absolute silence once the full moon begins. Dylan, Tempe, Dutch and Andy will form the center circle. The rest of us will be on the outer circle. Tempe, do you have River's new amphora?"

I reached into my leather satchel, removed the new one

and the one Jack returned to me earlier. "Is two better than one?"

She gave a deep sigh and nodded, "Yes, indeed."

Marty's voice broke the quiet again, "Don't forget the deadline for the derby is Saturday, Tempe."

"Hush, Marty," Aurora said under her breath. She frowned at the invisible Imp's location.

Okay, I wasn't the only one who could hear Marty? Had he spoken out loud that time? I could almost feel his contriteness, even without seeing him. "Yes'm, I'll go to my spot."

"Place the amphoras at the center of the inner circle," Aurora said.

Outside the larger one Dylan placed candles and cleansed the area with sage, frankincense and cinnamon. At 6:45 he lit white candles and stepped inside the outer circle taking his place next to me. Dutch and I were at East and West, Dylan and Andy, North and South. I had no idea where she'd put Marty. She then arranged everyone else on the outer circle and enclosed us all within a fine ring of salt.

Finally, it was time, but something we had not foreseen, a heavy band of clouds, moved across the sky obscuring the moon and leaving us with only the light from the candles and an increasing wind.

One candle was snuffed by the breeze, followed shortly by another. And another.

CHAPTER 15

TEMPE

Thur 7:48 pm "Ancient dudes—low tech."

ANDY OPENED his mouth but Aurora hissed, "Silence, Andy, until we're done. You should be concentrating on recent training sessions with River, anything that helps you keep him front and center in your mind." Directing her instructions to the rest of us, she said, "Get a clear image of River and do whatever you have to do to keep it there—memories, conversations, even arguments. One minute."

Flame jumped from the snuffed candles and steadied. All of the other flames followed suit. Several sets of eyes connected, curious. Since Aurora was directing and focusing the energies of the group, my money was on

Dutch. It would be a piece of cake for him to keep all the candles lit and still focus on River—*and* churn up an earthquake or three on top of that with any leftover energy.

I closed my eyes, searching my mind for memories of my brother. At first it was like slogging through deep mucky gumbo, my subconscious putting up barriers...

It's *to protect you from the pain, but I'm here, daughter...* Dutch's thoughts comforted, and his hand squeezed mine. Then the images flowed... *River running behind me on the grass, his little legs trying desperately to keep up, crying because I was going too fast. I turned and lifted him up high. His cries turning to giggles as he threw his arms up to the sky, wiggling his fingers, his curly bronze hair flopping in the wind as his squeals brought momma running.*

She plucked him from my arms and nuzzled his cheek. She was so happy and beautiful. "My little rolling River. You won't always be a trickle, baby boy." She commenced singing to him, lyrics she'd created just for us, "I once had a raindrop, drip, drop, drip, drop, but she became a Tempest. Then I had a trickle," she poked him in the belly, "tickle, trickle, tickle. But he trickled faster and faster until ooh, ooh, ooh, he turned into a River. Now Mommy has a tempest and river and she loves them thiiiiisss much," which ended in both of us being dropped into a mom-made pool of water. River's high squealing shrieks accompanied his splashing and kicking, drenching Phoebe and me.

It had been a wonderful day. I glanced at Dutch. Seeing my memory through the mindlink, he smiled and I returned it. My eyes closed and I made prayerful fists at my sides. This could work. I opened my thoughts searching for more family videos. And found Dutch trying to teach River how to start a fire, the Djinn method.

River sat across the pile of twigs and brush from our father who looked more relaxed and happy than I've ever seen him. "Okay, son, concentrate. You know what fire looks like, don't you?"

Three-year-old River nodded wide-eyed at Dutch. "Uh, yeah?"

Dutch chuckled and held his hand out palm up. "Like this." A tiny four-inch fire filled his hand, roaring and crackling just like the larger fireplace version.

River clapped and squealed. "Go, Daddy." Not to be outdone, Phoebe leaned over against Dutch and said, "Let me help you, darling, that must be hot," and conjured a tiny raincloud over his fire, complete with lightning and thunder. While River and I looked on they continued trying to one-up each other until we were all tired of the game and River was asleep in Dutch's lap. I leaned contentedly on one shoulder, Phoebe against his other.

It was the picture I'd seen at Phoebe's... I couldn't keep this up. I thought I would just find my most current memory of River at twenty-three and hold that, but I was hit by one after another tender childhood image which only made me ache to have my family restored, to have another chance. Phoebe woul—

Daughter, concentrate on River.

Fiery golden eyes captured mine. I inhaled, re-focused and did as he *suggested*.

The clouds cleared allowing the moon's light to spread across our circles for another thirty minutes. Dutch shifted abruptly and said, "It's not going to work."

"Wait," I said. The moon is still full—"

Aurora said, "He's right, Tempe. It's been an hour and a half. We should have connected fairly quickly."

I felt Jack move up behind me and slumped against him dejected. The others broke circle and picked up the candles and amphoras. "We still have time, honey. Aurora said this Para-moon thing isn't supposed to happen until Sunday or Monday, right, Aurora?"

Aurora sighed, "Yes. Jack's right, Tempe, we still have time."

Dutch faced Jack. "What we really need is *you people* to do your job and find out where they are holding him."

Furious, I pulled away from Jack and plowed my hands through my hair, "Cut it out with the 'you people'. We've been in this together for the last two weeks." Frustrated, I turned on Dutch. "Jack has worked as hard as anyone to find River—once he figured out I wasn't a murderer."

"Um, excuse me…" Jordie quietly squeezed in next to her father.

Jack said, "This is my daughter, Jordie, Dutch."

Dutch nodded formally and half smiled.

"What is it, Jordie?" I asked. She had that impatient air about her.

She frowned and scanned all our faces. "Well, if you're trying to find someone, why don't you try social media? Didn't you guys just take a class in it?"

"We never finished the class," muttered Jack.

We hadn't even thought about Squawker or Peeple Pages. Of course, our kind usually doesn't have to rely on human resources to solve our problems—especially social media. I guess it really is the Age of Aquarius. "What are you thinking, Jordie?"

"You could blast it to everyone in the area, looking for so-and-so and post her picture and River's. They do it all the time with missing children." She shrugged, "Just sayin'."

I looked at Aurora who looked at Jack. Dutch looked like he thought we'd lost our minds.

Jack said, "She's got a point. The reason I took the class was because it's become such a valuable tool in law enforcement. Aurora, do you know how to use Squawker or Peeple Pages?" At Aurora's needle-like he said, "Maybe I can get Peggy to do it. I've got the pictures on my phone but I don't remember my login or anything from class."

Andy looked at Jordie, "Old dudes, l-low t-t-tech."

Turning to her father Jordie said, "Text me the info and pictures. Andy and I will go to work on it." She motioned to Andy, "Let's go to my dad's car. It's cold out here." She looked at Andy and mouthed, *Ancient.*

She just didn't realize how close to the truth that was.

Jack

The universal language of fathers

I WATCHED Andy and Jordie through the windows of my cruiser. Just two days ago, I'd have adamantly opposed the idea of Jordie even knowing about the circle, much less be present, and yet, I'd allowed Aurora to talk me into it. Why? As it turned out, she'd been right, there'd been no danger, and more importantly, Jordie had been able to offer a solution with her idea about blasting the details on social media. I was like one of the family members now, hoping against hope something would come of it.

Tempe's friends milled around for almost an hour but the mood wasn't unlike the after-party at a wake. No one seemed to hold out much hope for River after the telepathy—the mindlink—failed. Montana and Kat tried to convince Tempe we'd find River, shooting me hopeful, and I'm sure they thought, instructive looks.

I wasn't getting, and didn't need, the *message.* I was doing everything I knew how to do. There were just no leads to go on. It was frustrating. In this part of the world there were so many old oil field roads and abandoned buildings and farms; the possibilities were endless.

I wasn't even sure River was alive but I didn't dare mention that to Tempe or Dutch. They wouldn't give up until...they just wouldn't. Unfortunately, in River's situation, the next two days were critical. After that, there would be no chance of finding him alive... unless, and this was even less palatable, he showed up under the control of the enemy.

Aurora, Dylan and Dutch stood near the back porch waiting on Tempe who had walked down to the bank of the bayou. Every few minutes the moon would peek through the clouds and shine down on her, the breeze making the strands of her hair look like waving Spanish moss. It gave a false illusion of serenity when I knew Tempe was grieving.

I didn't know how she continued to withstand the emotional hits that bombarded her. Her fear for River when she found he was missing after losing the rest of her family. Her mother leaving, her father re-appearing, the seeming betrayal of her friends and lover. How much more could she take? It's no wonder she'd lost it today, or I guess the correct phrase would be *found it*. Her power had finally shown up. And it had been amazing.

What had Dutch said? *You haven't seen nuclear.* Wow.

I walked toward the bayou. She seemed so alone, so lost. I was about to put my hands on her shoulders and lend my emotional support, but she fell against me as if she hadn't the strength to stand on her own. "I'm sorry it didn't work, sweetheart. Tell me what I can do for you."

The roar of the motorcycle starting up caused us both to jerk and turn around. Curious, Tempe frowned at her father's big Harley racing down the slope toward us. "What is he up to?" she muttered, but her words were lost in the thunderous approach of the bike.

Dutch came to a dusty stop a mere foot away and growled at Tempe, "Get on." His eyes were like bright teal and copper coins when he glared at me.

"What did *I* do?" I asked.

"Nothing," said Tempe. She turned and laid her hand against my cheek then kissed me on the lips as Dutch revved the engine like he was in some kind of bike club cockfight. "I'll be in touch."

She walked over to Dutch, swung her leg over the bike and twisted her hands in his tunic since there was no way she could reach around him. Dutch gunned the motor and spun the bike around, the back wheel sliding on the loose dirt and wet grass. I stood there watching as they disappeared over the top of the hill, the thundering sound of the big bike trailing behind it for a long time.

I was thirty-four years old, an ex-military commander, a sheriff and the father of a teenager, and my girlfriend's father had just interrupted what could have been an important *moment* by riding in on his Harley and ordering her to go with him.

144

Of all the things that came to mind, foremost was, *How much more... normal could things be?*

I shook my head and looked toward the Forge. When I looked back, Dylan stood next to me. With one dark brow arched he said, "Welcome to Destiny."

CHAPTER 16

JACK

Friday, 5:30 am Two kinds of crazy

AFTER A SLEEPLESS FEW HOURS, my head whirling with images from the last few days, I revisited the determination I'd made during the night. It was too dangerous for Jordie in this town. Especially after the call I'd received at 2 a.m. A domestic call, repeat offender.

The woman's husband or partner had been throwing furniture, breaking out windows. Her neighbor called 911 telling the dispatcher "her abuser needed to be put in jail for good this time. If not, she was going to wind up dead".

When we arrived on the scene, much of what I'd seen

up to that point had been theoretical, and the only POPs I'd met good guys. But this...

The house had been trashed. I would have expected this damage if the storm maiden had been inside in beast mode, the interior walls stripped of their paneling, lights hanging from wiring, windows busted, the victim lying in her own blood, barely alive. Strangest of all, there were scorch marks across the floor and up the wall, a set of bloody footprints on the floor as big around as a tree trunk. The creature responsible had walked through the blood and then disappeared. When I followed the soot on the wall, I looked up into an expanse of black sky and a million stars. The roof had been peeled back like the lid on a tin can.

The entire time I'd been searching the room, a tiny mouse had darted from wall to wall frantic to find an escape. Afraid of what I would do, but it was *just* a mouse. I opened the front door. It stopped as it crossed the threshold, stared up at me with... no forget it, I am totally losing it. The last I saw of the little rodent was when the ambulance arrived outside and it took off across the yard. Free at last, I thought, then caught sight of a scrap of delicate red fabric. The undergarment had looked so out of place in the scene but I'd collected it to keep it from being trampled. It was evidence after all.

The injured woman had given me a statement. It sounded like, "The dinch saved me. Tanker."

What the hell did that mean?

As I looked in the mirror I wondered, where was my resolve? I'd made my decision just hours ago and here I was vacillating again. Who could blame me? In the last three days, I'd found out that not only did my soon-to-be girlfriend brew up storms when she got mad, but her father and brother were genies.

Genies. If I said it again, out loud, maybe it would sink in. "G-e-n-i-e." Then there was the local B&B. Now I knew why it was supposedly always booked. It was owned by the Green Giant and his Queen, and there was a whole lot more weird going on there.

I'd been jealous of *Diablo,* my chosen handle for McGuinness, the first time I'd met the investigator and suspected he was Tempe's ex-lover. I'd actually related to his dressed in black, ex-Special Forces persona, but since then I'd met his inner Sasquatch, twice, and the jury's still out as to whether I'm more intimidated, or jealous. Probably the latter.

Add the newest revelation, the Pomeroys speak to each other with their minds. These were not things I could discuss with anyone from my... what should I call it... previous life... other life? I couldn't begin to imagine how my parents would react if they ever found out.

I rubbed the grit out of my eyes. Dutch and Tempe had driven the streets on that big Harley all night. Even though Dutch told Tempe he'd given up on the mindlink, I'd seen the pain in his eyes. Genies probably don't need to sleep so I wasn't surprised when they were spotted in nearly every neighborhood from North of town to the South, and complaints came in over the thundering of that bike from the state park near Amity to the winding country roads near Alliance. I wondered if it had been just the bike *thundering*.

My earlier antagonism of Tempe's father had been based on a contrived background and on the very real pain his deception had caused Tempe. I'd revised my opinion of him after finding out the reason he'd faked his death, which was evidence of his devotion to his children. But the man... Djinn... whatever, was—I pinched myself again—yep, still here sitting in my bed with Jordie in the other room... Dutch was *thousands* of years old.

I shook my head. How could I keep Jordie in this environment? Giving my daughter stable, 'normal' surroundings to grow up in without a lot of the craziness she'd had to endure early in her life had been my Prime Objective. Unfortunately, this town epitomized *crazy*.

Sure, Jordie had handled the "seance" or whatever Aurora had named the gathering with remarkable composure, but what would she do when she found out some if not all of the people she knew weren't... human? When she saw Dutch or Tempe or *Dylan* in action? Would she turn into the rebel she'd avoided so far? Run away? God forbid, go live with her mother, wherever *she* was?

Well, there was nutty and strange, and then there was deranged, like my ex. That was my answer.

Things might be *different* here, but it was Jordie's mother's stunts that were unjustified, unbearable, and unacceptable. Like the two years she claimed to have a job on the road in sales and had left Jordie with my parents, only appearing once and even then, by accident.

I'd hired a private investigator in advance of my custody suit. He described the company she'd kept with words like *strange, slimy, low-lifes, dumpster-diving scavengers* and even the word *creature* had been thrown about. He'd never offered me photos or detailed descriptions but it had been enough for me to start the proceedings against her for abandonment.

My breath pushed out as I swung my legs over the side of the bed. Right now, if I had to pick one environment over another I'd pick the caring individuals I'd met in Destiny hands down. Case in point, Tempe had been on the run, and she still took time to make sure my daughter was safe. Jordie had asked Tempe to come to her game, and she'd not only showed up but brought half the town with her to sit in Jordie's section on game night.

A lot had happened since I asked Tempe to go to the Mardi Gras ball with me. With only thirty-six hours left before the ball, it looked like I was going to be disappointed. I could live with that if we found River. But who knew what could happen between now and then?

I reached for my toothbrush. Did the man who faced me in the mirror look any different? Did I *feel* different? I met the steady green eyes of my ego. *Yes*, I decided. I felt alive and even with everything I'd learned in the last couple weeks, and the impending problems, I felt the enticing pull of excitement. I'd faced the same thing in my Navy career. Challenge. Like the forces of the world betting against you but you believe you can conquer whatever it throws at you. *Yeah.* I was up for it.

"Jordie," I called down the hallway. "Time to get up." Beffie, the non-dog, loped down the hall to—in a perfect imitation of a real canine—lick my hand and woof.

I looked into those intelligent eyes. "Good, d—whatever you are. You can stick around as long as Jordie wants you, or until you get another 'job'." The creature answered with another *bark* and I let him out to do whatever faerie guard dogs do.

JACK

1 pm What good's a genie that can't wish?

WE NEEDED MORE time but we weren't going to get it. Every time I looked at my watch we were that much closer to the next full moon and yet *another* critical juncture.

The other parishes and towns reported in with no results. When I saw Tempe at Gators Grub at lunch showing River's picture to some tourists, I could tell she'd about given up hope. She'd been up all night and was wearing the same clothes she'd been in when Dutch took off with her. "Have you had any sleep?" I asked.

She stumbled and practically fell into my arms, leaning against me, a heavy sigh breathed against my chest. "I can't sleep when…" her voice trailed off. I supported her with my arms wrapped around her and let her rest for a couple minutes. I was past the point of worrying about holding her in public. Everyone knew Tempe was about tapped out. Even Dick the flower man didn't give her a second look. That said a lot. He must figure the news about River wasn't going to be good.

I'd been surprised at the number of people who'd come out and volunteered to beat the bushes—literally—going through the government CRP land, acres of thick young tree growth, with dogs and sticks, braving the snakes and mosquitoes to look for River. There were former customers of River's, even Max; college buddies, mail carriers, and lots of Tempe's customers; some taking an active part, others just offering her support or passing out flyers. You couldn't turn down any street or highway around Storm Lake without seeing River's likeness on a pole or in a window.

By this time I was fairly sure when we did find him it was going to be when they stumbled across his body—if genies even left remains behind when they *died*. I didn't want to ask that question. Or, there'd be a development and we'd have to mount an emergency rescue operation to get him away from his captors. That breakthrough came late in the afternoon.

Peggy contacted me by radio and gave me two messages. "You must have been out of service. Aurora and Jordie both called."

I pulled into a convenience store and called Aurora first, curious to see if she knew anything but she just wanted me to know the gown I'd ordered for Tempe was here. "Jack, I believe we'll find River, and you need to believe it as well, for Tempe's sake as well as River's."

"Aurora, if this were a purely..." I pressed the heel of my hand to my forehead and squeezed my eyes shut. "If this were a 'human' case, and we'd run out of our leads like we have here, the search would have been suspended. The extenuating circumstances differ because of what you've called a global threat."

"That's exactly right, Jack. I know you're still uncomfortable with much that you've seen—"

I barked a laugh then sobered and came clean with Aurora. "I don't want to have to be the one to tell Tempe that River—"

Aurora *said, "Shush,* Jack. You've been good for her. I know you've dealt with some harsh realities in your life and at work, but don't give up on River."

What did she know about my life? Had Jordie been talking about her mother? I couldn't help but be curious. "I'll talk to you later."

"Remember, Jack—believe."

"Yeah. Right." If wishes could only make it so. Come to

think of it, why couldn't Dutch just wish up River's location? Oh right, the personal restriction to wish granting. I shook my head and pulled up my phone favorites.

Jordie's ringtone sounded before I could call her back, and her excited squeal grabbed my attention.

"Daddy, we've found something on Squawker. I got a DS from an elderly lady, Ms. Elaine Johnson."

"What's a DS?" I frowned and dug my pad out of my coat pocket.

She sighed, "A direct squawk. Anyway, Mrs. Johnson said there's been some suspicious activity at an abandoned deer camp on her road. She doesn't have TV or radio, just a cell phone. She gave me her number and the directions, and I have her Squawker handle if you can't reach her by phone."

I wrote the information down. "What makes you think this is the place, Jordie?"

"Because she recognized Will Crain's truck, the red pickup with equipment in the back?"

"Sweetheart, I… owe… you, big time."

I heard her delight through the phone. "That's affirmative, Daddy-o."

I called the cell phone number but it went directly to a voicemail box that hadn't been set up. "Damn!" I got my dispatcher on the radio. "Peggy, are you familiar with a road near Hutchins Lane?" I gave her the address.

"There are several old oilfield locations out that way, boss. Most of them were abandoned twenty-five years ago."

I filled her in. "I want you to keep calling this woman and get as much detail as you can. See if she has any family in town. Contact each of our deputies on their cells, and keep it off the scanner. Don't let any of our people go near there. When we go, we want to be sure who's on that road. If she calls, patch her through to my cell. I've got to make some calls."

I called Ryan first because he was the only one I could trust to stake out the road discreetly. "I want you to see if there's a way to get the old woman out of there without being seen or drawing suspicion. I've got Peggy checking on family as well. Get out there, and you and Peggy stay in touch by phone only."

"Roger that." After tonight Ryan would probably be taking off for the other side of the world.

I called Tempe. She answered before I heard a ring. "What?"

"Tempe, we have a lead. A good one. I'll meet you at Harmony. Keep it to yourself."

*J*ACK

THE EXCITEMENT in Tempe's dining room was palpable. Tempe paced running hands through her hair. "I hate the waiting, now that we know. We have to get to him."

Dutch wrapped one Hulk-ish arm around her shoulders and said, "Your sheriff is right to be sure, Tempest. We can't go off half..." he frowned.

"Half-cocked," I offered, encouraged by the 'your sheriff'. "No, we can't. Not when we're this close, Tempe. We need to isolate the area and make a plan."

Dutch kept his gaze steady on me but released Tempe. She walked over to me. "Do you think we'll be in time?"

I swallowed, looking at Dutch. His eyes were sad, but I saw the faint stirrings of hope in them. I pulled her to me, and damned if the big Djinni didn't turn away. Quoting Aurora I said, "You have to believe, Tempest Pomeroy. After all you've been through, it couldn't have been for nothing."

Dutch turned at that and met my eyes. I met his right back. "You and Phoebe put her through a lot. If this were the old world I might have challenged you to a dual." I raised a hand when I saw the heat in his eyes. "I know you thought you were doing the right thing, the only thing you *knew* to do, but you put Tempe through hell."

Dutch cleared his throat. "I'm sorry, daughter. If I had known..."

"Can we *not* do this right now?" asked Tempe, pushing

out of my embrace. A knock sounded on the door and it opened as Dylan, Kat and Montana entered. I looked down to see that same Dachshund, the one who "belonged to a friend". *Right.*

I narrowed a look at Tempe. "Another faerie dog?"

The Dachshund changed in front of my eyes into one of the ugliest— "What *is* that—he?"

The creature spoke, and though he was less than a foot tall, straightened into a dignified posture and managed to put head shake into his scratchy voice. "Marty is me name. I was River's familiar, actually, the family familiar. My good looks aside, I may be able to be of some help."

Good looks? I let that slide since he obviously judged his looks by a different set of guidelines than I was familiar with. Ha, familiar, pun.

So, I included the wrinkly mud colored little guy as I filled Dylan, Kat and Montana in on our situation. Montana said, "If you need to get Mrs. Johnson out of there, Rafe and I could go in the ambulance. You could create an emergency call and even broadcast it on the scanner in case they're listening. We'll take her out on the gurney so no one would be suspicious."

"That's a good plan, Montana. You might even go ahead and use the sirens to announce your presence and make sure they don't think its some kind of trick because there's no way you'll get in and out without them seeing you."

"Good idea," Dylan said. "Might lull them into complacence after they leave with Mrs. Johnson."

Tempe said, "That's why all the flyers and newspaper announcements didn't work. And the road is on the far side of the bayou so Dylan didn't pick up the scent. Have you heard from Ryan yet, Jack?" Tempe asked.

"He's got the deer camp in his sights. Will's truck *is* there and so is Paige's car."

"*Zeus bouncing bolts*! Finally!" Tempe bent over as relief surged through her. Montana rubbed her shoulder.

"Peggy has Mrs. Johnson's son at the office. She had to assure him we'd get his mother out of there safely and soon. I promised I'd call him in thirty minutes with our plan."

Montana pulled her cell phone out. "I'll go ahead and put Rafe on standby. We'll go when you say the word."

I faced Tempe's father. "Dutch, do you have both amphoras?"

"Yes, but you know we can't use the old one for River."

"I remember you mentioned that," I said. "But tell me why again?" His answer would mean the difference in my plan working or not.

Dutch went into an explanation about the power of a Djinni's force and the need for architectural integrity in a bottle. "It wouldn't work for containment." I repeated.

"Or protection," Dutch said.

"What about as a backup or *temporary* vessel?" I asked.

Dutch sat back, his golden gaze considering.

"I take it you have a plan," Dylan said.

I gave Tempe's hand a squeeze. "I have an idea. Dutch will have to decide if it will work."

Tempe

5:20pm

I WATCHED through binoculars as Montana and Rafe drove down the dusty gravel road, lights flashing and pulled up to the Johnson home, next to the son's Ford Focus. Jack had changed the plan thinking it would look less suspicious if the call came from her son to 911 and was picked up on the scanner. He was fairly sure Paige and Will had been keeping track of police movement on a police scanner. Jack set up some phony police calls between Peggy and Basile and even a fake "lead" they were following, supposedly in Amity.

Ten interminable minutes later, they had Mrs. Johnson on the gurney and a worried looking son hurriedly jumped into his car and followed the ambulance. I silently thanked him for following Jack's instructions to the letter, not once looking down the road or over his shoulder. Now came the critical part of the plan.

At various locations around the perimeter of the rural "block" were Dylan, Marty and Kat. Jack had asked what good Kat would be against desperate criminals. Funny, he didn't ask about Marty. Ugly must translate to dangerous. I assured him that even though he'd seen Katerina dressed in black, he hadn't seen her "darkest" side. He'd merely nodded, synced our watches for his 6:10 appointment with Paige, and sent them off to guard the back of the property against an unlikely escape by either Will or Paige.

Ryan sat ready as backup on the road's entrance, in case either Paige or Will somehow got past the rest of us. The unexpected happened at 6:05 pm. A single gunshot rang out.

CHAPTER 17

TEMPE

My sinkhole of a life

JACK REACHED FOR HIS GUN, eyeing the cabin. Angry sparks danced in front of my eyes as I struggled to keep from running to River's rescue.

Dutch's voice rumbled, "Was this part of your plan?" He sounded as if he might blow any minute. I glanced over at him and decided that was an accurate assessment. Jack noticed, too.

"There are two possibilities. An internal shift of power between Will and Paige, or..."

I took that to mean either Will had shot Paige or vice versa, or River had tried to overpower them and failed, which wasn't likely in the shape he was in. "What are you going to do?" I asked as Jack walked around the car toward the cabin.

"I'm going to find out."

I grabbed his arm. My world seemed to be one big sink-hole where the people I loved kept falling into the pit. My mouth was so dry all I could do was whisper, "Please, Jack... be careful."

He put his hand on my neck, his gaze narrowed on mine. "I haven't given up on River yet and neither should you. We work the plan."

Dutch's hands settled on my shoulders. Jack looked at him. "Give me fifteen minutes before you approach, unless you hear another gunshot. If you do, bring it on —Genies, Tempestaeries, Sasquatch, whatever—other-wise, wait for me to signal you."

My stomach was in knots as I watched Jack disappear around the last stand of trees, just a few yards from the cabin. Dutch said, "Stay here, Tempest. I will make sure your man doesn't come to harm."

"To hell with that!" I hissed. "Let's go."

JACK

THE CABIN, what was left of it, was worse than run-down, the walls so full of holes it was a wonder the structure could support even a dilapidated roof. I looked at the sagging porch and rotted steps. It wouldn't take a Tempestaerie to blow this house down. One good puff from Destiny's resident Finrir would probably do it.

But it had served its purpose in hiding River's where-abouts until now, being nearly invisible in the overgrown forest. I could feel eyes on me, whether they were from inside or our people—*huh, a Freudian slip of the tongue*. My neck prickled with the sixth sense that had saved my ass many a time in the air. I decided on the direct approach.

"Hello, the cabin. Sheriff's Office. Paige Whyte, if you're in there, we need to talk."

I made another step and a voice rang out through the crack in the front door. "I saw you, Sheriff. Where are your men?"

I turned as if I'd forgotten about my "men" and looked back at the cabin. "I don't have any men, Ms. Whyte. It's just me." Showing respect might get me in, where aggressiveness might not.

She seemed to be thinking about my statement and was probably looking for my backup in the distance, but except for the gravel street where I stood, there was little to see. My deputies' vehicles were over a mile away. "How about you let me in, Paige? I might be able to help you get what you want."

She was thinking again and no sounds of voices or shuffling escaped the cabin.

"Why would you want to help me?" Paige asked. Still no sign of Will; she must be calling the shots, which made sense, her being the one with some *slight* power.

"Eh, it's one of those 'you scratch my back, I'll scratch yours' situations. We just need to discuss what it is you want and we can make a deal, something we can both live with."

"Leave your gun outside. Put it on the ground in front of you, very slowly. And don't try anything. I have a pistol pointed right at you."

I didn't doubt it. I did as she instructed. "What now?" I asked, letting her think she was in control.

"Turn around." I did. Once satisfied she said, "Now come up on the porch." I heard the lock on the door being released. "I'm going to back away from the door. When you come in, stay on that side of the room. Don't try to rush me or come near me."

"Fine," I said and walked toward the door, testing my weight on each rickety step before moving up to the next. I had to push hard on the door, the rusty hinges groaning and squeaking. The cabin was dimly lit from a lantern in the corner on the floor. In the waning light, the lantern cast odd shadows on everything, including Paige's face, making her look like a ghost.

While her eyes were still adjusting from the sudden flood of outside light, I made a quick search of the large main room. There was a door near the corner on her right. Bathroom or bedroom? The main area was sparsely furnished with a twin mattress shoved against the other front wall; a milk crate upended for a table sat beside a plastic lawn chair, with a huge circular oak table to my right. I tapped my fingers on the edge of it. It was sturdy, and a scanner sat on the other side. I heard the phony messages going back and forth between my men.

Still no sign of Will Crain, but on a couch on the other side of the oak table, two feet from Paige, lay River Pomeroy. If he *was* alive, it wouldn't be for long. His skin was like ash and he was as frail and limp as the newly embalmed. His once burgundy shirt was covered in dust, and the pants showed signs of his being dragged. I didn't see his chest rising or any eyelid movement from where I was standing.

I tried to come up with a strategy but without knowing more about that gunshot, where her partner in crime was, and who might be in the other room, I was left with simply keeping my back to the wall where I had a full view of Paige and her gun.

Her clothes were disheveled, her blonde hair tangled and greasy, eyes moving back and forth frenetically. A large hank of hair had been cut, or ripped, from her red abraded scalp. The hand that wasn't on the gun held some kind of cord attached to River.

"What's wrong with River?"

She raised the gun, held it steady, as if she had experience. Her voice held contempt. "Why do you think I need *you*? I don't. I want Dutch!" Spittle flew with her words. "Get Dutch, and you can leave. And where's that witch?"

I assumed she meant Tempe. There was certainly no love lost here. Paige fidgeted, not with nerves, more like a drug addict in need of a fix. Could she be on something?

I tried a different tack. "Answer me, Paige. What did you give River?"

She made a guttural sound and rubbed the handle of the gun against her forehead but not long enough for me to make a move. In a gravelly, slow voice she said, "I don't have to answer your questions. I don't *need* you."

When she shifted, the meager light illuminated the tether. It was made of *hair*—braided hair. Then I noticed the similar patch on River's scalp. The cord connecting her to River was some kind of hair leash. *I hadn't seen it all yet apparently.* What was its purpose? Was it keeping him passive, or keeping him alive? My guess was the latter. Damn, this complicated matters.

I answered, keeping my voice steady, "If you kill me, Dutch won't find you. You chose your hiding place very well, Paige—you and Will, and they've been unable to contact River." Again, this time making no attempt to hide my curiosity, I cast my glance around the room looking for Crain. "If I hadn't been driving down this road when the ambulance came through, I'd have never known to check this place out." I intentionally looked at the scanner, making sure she caught it. "You were listening on the scanner weren't you?"

"How do I know you didn't bring others with you?" she snarled.

"Did you hear me call for backup? I didn't think there was anyone in this old death trap. I would have called but there's no reception out here... look." She backed up a step when I held my phone out, turning it around so she could see the *no service* message displayed on the screen.

"Why would you get Dutch for me?" she asked, suspiciously.

I put as much distaste in my voice as I could drum up. "I don't really care what you Paramortal people do as long as you leave my town alone." Her posture improved when she thought I viewed her as a Paramortal— someone she obviously felt had power over others, a state of power she wanted for herself. "We'll make a deal. I get you what you want and you leave, go off to the other side of the world, New York or China for all I care, where you have a bigger population to *harass*."

Paige seemed to consider that and calling her a Paramortal had earned me a few points, or at least bought me some time.

She looked over at River then back at me. "What do you want?" She was having trouble keeping a smile off her face now, her eyes wily and bright with a greedy fever. She didn't intend to keep her part of any bargain; I knew it. The only deal this bad POP would make would be one that ensured she got Dutch in her control so she could wield all the power she'd been denied. On top of any minimal power she might have, I was dealing with a classic inferiority complex with a little psychopathic narcissism thrown in.

"I want answers. And after I get Dutch for you, you leave… immediately," I reiterated.

Paige considered how she could manipulate me, her plan racing around in her head like dragsters. Her irises were large shimmering gray orbs. Did she have more power than before, and did she have a *menori* inside like Tempe?

I heaped coals on the fire. "Come to think of it, I may not need to deal with you. I heard you were a miniscule tempest faerie, that you have no real power." My ploy worked.

Paige's temper flared, and I saw it coming a split second before a jolt of white heat struck my thigh, sending sparks from my phone and pain radiating through my nerve endings. I let the phone fall onto the table and leaned on it, gasping, not entirely for effect. It hurt like hell. I didn't try to hide it, instead making it seem worse than it was. I'd been tasered a couple of times in the military and once in Memphis; those times paled in comparison. No negligible faerie here.

"What did you do, get more power from River?" I said, panting hard.

She laughed but the smile was evil. "At your daughter's game last week, River's stupid Djinn protégé was dishing out free wishes to anyone within range. I had Will make a wish for me. But the damn squid blew it by simply wishing for a *little* more..." her voice trailed off when she realized she was about to admit to gaining only a limited amount of power. "I've felt..." she turned it on, her eyes brightening and her shoulders twitching "...different, *stronger* since then. *Much* more powerful."

And *much* less sane.

"So what happened, Paige? What was the plan? How did it all go wrong?"

I leaned my hip against the oak table, rubbing my thigh. I hoped her zapper was out of juice. She'd reacted to her mad like Tempe had before she knew how to control her power, back when only emotion ruled its course and strength. Tempe told me when I'd first met her it took hours for her force to recharge. Hopefully, it was the same for Paige.

"Come on, Paige. Start anywhere. When did you decide to steal the amphora from Tempe's?"

Paige's disjointed answer was an indication of how fast she was slipping. "This whole fiasco is all the Nucklavee's fault. If he hadn't taken the bartender's place that Saturday at the Turtle... He revealed his true self to me that night and asked if I wanted more power, to be more like Phoebe Pomeroy, even *take her* power." Her hand came palm up, and she stared at it, "I could have storms *here* at my command."

Emotion stirred in her eyes again and I prayed she'd keep it together. I wasn't looking forward to another jolt. "So that's when you planned to take the amphora?"

Her hand tightened on the gun, "*No!*" Agitated again. We didn't steal the damned bottle. The Nuk had a plan to capture Phoebe. He wanted to kidnap River and use him to lure Tempe and Phoebe in. He had me text River and tell him I had information about one of her protectors. But the real Ray found out and the other two left with Phoebe. The Nuk gave me a drug to put in River's beer or whatever he ordered. I know how strong he is, so I doubled the dose."

Obviously, that hadn't been a good decision. She kicked at something on the floor and glared into the ether. Maybe she'd get into her tale and forget where she was, give me an opening.

"The Nucklavee was furious. River was going under too fast. Will and I told him we'd make it look like he couldn't wait to go somewhere private to 'get it on'. He was just conscious enough that he could walk with me supporting him and it didn't take much to make it look like he was all over me." She looked up, her eyes clouded over, "Like he used to be."

Everything I'd learned about River pointed to *that* being a lie. "Will described a brunette and at least one person backed that up."

"Easy. A costume wig from Halloween City. That's all." She waved the gun.

"Not hardly. If you didn't take River's amphora, who did?"

For a minute I thought she wouldn't answer but I realized she needed to tell it all. She just wanted me to beg. "Come on, Paige."

"After Will and I brought River to the cabin and Ray—the Nuk—couldn't find him, he decided to steal the amphora. Without the amphora," she hesitated wondering what I knew—

"—You couldn't contain River's force."

"Yes, and without River, the Nuk couldn't make his boss' plan work. Nuks aren't smart enough to do anything on their own, you know."

I nodded, even though this was all *breaking news* to me.

"Who was his boss?"

"Someone… very powerful." Her smile died, fear reflected plainly on her features. "You interrupted me." Again she rubbed her forehead with the gun. "Where was I? Oh, right. By then we'd heard Dutch was back in circulation, and *he* is the big prize. The Nuk didn't care about Phoebe anymore, and Tempe's a nothing," she said with a wealth of disdain. "No power except those ridiculous little mini-storms." She waved dismissively.

She obviously hadn't heard about Tempe's newfound

cyclone-ness. "So Ray, the Nucklavee, stole the amphora from Harmony and took it to the clubhouse where he took the real Ray's place. Why?" I scratched my head and tried to look confused, because things were falling into place.

"The Nucklavee took Ray's place after Ray didn't lead him to Phoebe. He shifted into his likeness and used Ray's keys to get into the clubhouse where he put River's bottle into one of the lockers. Will followed him, and as soon as he returned to the front room, Will surprised him, attacking him with a club he found in Ray's cleaning closet and searched him. He didn't find the amphora, but he found a small vial of that poison in the Nuk's pocket. He knew the cops would be coming because of the alarm but he didn't expect Tempest Pomeroy. She came blundering in there calling for the manager and Will panicked. At least he thought to grab the club and the vial since they had his fingerprints on them." She clucked, "Still, he's an idiot."

"Where is Will?"

Paige pointed to the floor on the other side of the table with the gun.

I leaned to the left to see Will lying in a pool of his own blood. "Is he dead?"

Before I could react, she pointed the gun down at Will's body, and pulled the trigger. I tensed, preparing myself for the inevitable.

She moved the gun back in my direction and the

deranged look returned. Her stare was cold, deadly. "He is now."

Pointing the gun at my heart, she said, "Quit stalling. I've answered your questions and unless you fulfill your part of the bargain *now!*—" her voice dropped menacingly "—you'll end up like Will."

Paige was like one of those biorhythm charts, only the highs and lows were bouncing through the top of the chart. The new increase in her power had obviously unhinged her.

Muttering, she said, "All of this talk has been rather unburdening—" She circled the hand with the gun mimicking a rising euphoric cloud but stopped short, looking me over. Apparently realizing I didn't have the bottle to make this deal happen, she said, "If you don't have the amphora, hidden in your back pocket, you're dead anyway."

Think fast, Jack—

But before I could respond, the roaring began.

CHAPTER 18

Jack

Friday, 6:40pm Thunder rolls…

A CRACKLING NOISE like fire sputtering in the hearth when new tinder is applied preceded the entry of a foggy image, which took form in front of us. "Did I hear my name?" came the words from a colossal gray miasma of gases.

Paige shivered involuntarily, her fist tightening on the tether and pulling it taut. "Don't try anything. I'm all that's keeping him alive." She pointed the gun at River and Dutch's thickening image surged forward.

I yelled, "No, Dutch. She means it." I pointed at Crain's body on the floor. The undulating, roiling mass paused, like a time-lapsed cloud video set on repeat, but he remained stationary as he considered his options. For a father who wanted to preserve his son's life, there weren't many, even if he *was* the most "powerful Djinn" known. His hands were tied, as well as his wishes.

Dutch's eyes were molten fire blazing at Paige's words, his voice echoing off the walls like the bass register of an organ in a celestial cathedral. I wasn't sure the flimsy walls could withstand much at that level. "Harming him wouldn't be very smart at this point, *Aretuu*."

I knew that word. Enemy. Did it apply to Paige?

"I w-was just s-saying…" With wide eyes she stepped even closer to River, her finger winding another loop around the hair leash, tethering his force to her weak one.

She cowered under Dutch's hulking presence. He leaned closer and though her eyes widened, she had the presence of mind, or self-preservation, to stick the gun in River's side, making her point.

He made a growl that felt like thunder and I stepped in before one of them blew a gasket. "Here's what I propose, Paige." I pulled River's old amphora from my waistband under my jacket. There was an immediate flare of interest on her face. "I have River's amphora and the other lid, which we found at Will's this morning. Dutch, if Paige promises to let me take River out of here, are you willing to get in this amphora and become the subject of the new possessor?"

Irritated beyond measure, Dutch glared at Paige, his

eyes blazing, skin glowing like embers on a log. She cowered next to River waiting for his answer. The massive being turned and his burning eyes narrowed on me. Even though we'd worked some of this out ahead of time, I had to wonder, seeing his wrath up close and personal, and feeling only a fraction of the Djinn's thrumming power, if he would be able to follow through with the plan. How much intelligence remained when he was in this state?

A mere nod, almost undetectable, bound the Djinn to the oath as surely as the chains of Zeus. I let out a quick breath of relief and picked up the green amphora, holding it out so Paige could see that one opening was plugged. I held up the other hat-shaped lid.

Like an industrial vacuum cleaner sucking smoke out of a room, Dutch's dark foggy visage disappeared into the amphora, the rest evaporating like a vapor trail from my F-18 engines. Carefully, I placed it into the remaining spout, and sealed the Djinni inside.

Paige's excitement was palpable as she rocked from foot to foot. "Give me that amphora. Now!"

"No. I have to take River out of here. That was the deal. Let River go." Tempe had better make her move or I would have to wing it.

Her hand tightened around the tether. "Hand me the bottle…"

Wind blew leaves against the panes of glass, and limbs struck the roof of the house sending acorns and other trash skittering across the tin and down into the cabin. Paige paid little attention, her greedy eyes locked on the amphora in my hand. A deep rolling grumble shook the house as lightning cracked and reflected off the walls like blue spears.

"Give me the amphora," she snarled.

I stared her down. "Release River first."

There was a sound like a giant's foot slamming the ground—once... twice. The foundation rocked. I struggled to keep my balance and to keep the amphora level in my grip. But the house shook again, and I was tossed to the floor. Then the paneling in the walls buckled.

JACK

Don't try this at home...

PAIGE SHOUTED, "That's not a tornado. That's his spawn." She yelled toward the ceiling. "You might as well stop, Tempest. I'm not letting River leave until I get the amphora."

A tree slammed sideways into the house and we both jumped. But the winds quieted and Paige reached out, "Give it to me."

"Release him first. You heard Dutch take the oath. All of his power will be yours if you drop the leash and if you decided not to abide by our agreement, you could always take the amphora from me."

Her eyes narrowed as she considered my words. Finally, she relinquished her hold on River, the hair braid falling to the wood floor. His form instantly looked less substantial. As she reached toward me, an ashy cloud burst through the wall and a hand of fire plucked the bottle from the space where her hand had been. The fire-rimmed mass resembled the thundering black clouds of a volcanic eruption, the edges a roiling tumult billowing toward the ceiling.

Eyes of brilliant orange fire turned on Paige and one broad sweep of a sooty gray *hand* slammed her across the room into the far wall to crumple onto the body of Will Crain. The edges of the cloud beast faintly resembled a woman as she bent over the amphora, cradling it in paws of diaphanous soot. Lightning flickered continually along the edges of the molten clouds.

Once again, it seemed I watched a National Geographic playback of volcanic destruction, villages swept away by lava, lava that was perilously close to dripping off those limbs and wreaking havoc on the cabin. Her volcanic storm woman was even more incredible than the cyclone-kid fighting with her father.

But within seconds, her smoky hair took on the familiar streaks of turquoise, teal and silver. The lid of the amphora plopped off the top of the bottle and Dutch's greasy gray vapor oozed from it, spreading out into the massive shape of an angry PaPa Djinn. I could relate.

With an anguished cry he solidified at River's bedside, a copper hulk once again, taking in his son's condition. "Tempest, bring fire," he ordered.

The volcanic Tempe sizzled across the floor, leaving a burning path on the old cypress planks. She stood next to Dutch, her gaze only once going to the crumpled form of Paige, the edges of her charcoal nimbus burning brighter with rage. Dutch spoke again, grabbed a handful of her Vulcan heated cloud form and pulled her down toward River.

"He needs your fire now, Tempest."

The hulking volcano woman *knelt* by her brother's side. As Dutch pressed on River's diaphragm and released, the maw of the fire creature opened and spewed a straight stream of fire directly into the younger man's mouth.

What the hell? Djinni mouth to mouth? "Don't try that at home."

Father and daughter turned their heads toward me, the copper colored Djinni and the fiery thunder maiden, their pupils both vertical golden flames.

"Good," Dutch rumbled. "That will hold him until I can get him to a healer."

The creature nodded over River and turned to "look" at me. I assumed that's what was going on. It—she still didn't have what I called eyes but I got the sense she could see and understand.

Dutch laid his massive paw on her... smoke. "Do you need help getting back to your human form, Sweetie?"

There were a lot of things I hadn't considered funny about this whole fiasco as bizarre as it had been, but this just took the cake, calling a ten foot tall volcanic creature of thunder clouds and fire—*sweetie*. The sheer relief from the enormity of recent weeks' revelations erupted out of me in a paroxysm of laughter.

I tried to get a grip but I didn't seem to be able to latch onto anything of any urgency. No outstanding life or death issues, nothing needing my immediate attention, so I gave into my week knees and sagged against the wall, uncharacteristic breathy puffs continuing to bleed out.

Until I heard a heavy, stern voice say, "Sorry to interrupt your breakdown, Sheriff, but would you please call Dylan and tell him to collect these two?" I looked up to see Tempe and Dutch bending over me, heads together, similar frowns on their faces.

"Sorry," I said, wiping tears from my eyes and feeling another minor surge of hysteria. Dutch gave me a hand up and nearly sent me through the far wall.

"At least you're laughing," muttered Tempe, who was back to my gorgeous flame-haired lady.

*J*ACK

10:12 pm I'm missing something...

I LET myself into the house. Beffie met me at the door, and then loped back to Jordie's room. I checked on her and headed for the shower. Tempe had been sad and completely exhausted when I'd dropped her off at Harmony. Montana and Katerina had met me there, so I left her in their hands. They assured me she'd be okay after they plied her with "a glass" of wine. Talk about zero tolerance.

I'd reminded her about the Grand Ball and given her a chance to back out but she looked at me and said, "You're not getting out of it, Jack Lang. It's been the bright spot in my week. The anticipation helped give me hope that things were going to turn out okay with River. After everything that's happened, I'd think you'd be looking forward to a regular old costume party, even if it *is* the weirdest one of the year. The Mardi Gras Ball serves up some surprises but they aren't usually life-changing."

"I certainly hope not," I said. I'd had enough surprises to last a lifetime.

Tempe said she planned to go for her dress fitting as soon as Aurora opened Saturday morning. Anticipation lanced like a laser to my groin when I thought about stripping her out of that dress after the ball. I couldn't deny I'd had that thought many times since meeting my sexy mail lady.

Scrubbing my skin with the washcloth I ran back over the last two weeks. Jack "Laser" Lang was a completely different man than when he'd arrived in Destiny. I was still a sheriff, still a father, my military career and everything in my life was still the same and yet, it was all new. It would take some time for it to sink in but I was no longer thinking of leaving Destiny just because it was... *unique*. So the people around me, even my prospective girlfriend were more than human —that's how I preferred to look at it. They weren't criminals. They were good people. Some of them could just *do stuff*. I figured I could live with that. And hadn't I just decided this morning that security for Jordie and a bit of excitement for me weren't mutually exclusive?

Something kept niggling at me... I wracked my brain but just couldn't dredge it out of the tired muck. I lay down on the bed. As my mind slowed nearing sleep, I remembered—it was what Aurora had said, about the Para-moon and loss of power. I reminded myself to ask them about it tomorrow. Hadn't Aurora said the big day would be Monday or Tuesday? I drifted off. I had to get some sleep even if the world blew up tomorrow. Which wasn't likely.

Tempe

8:21 pm Love of a lifetime

JACK WALKED out with Dylan and the still unconscious Paige to give Dutch and me a few minutes alone.

"Dutch—"

He let out an exasperated sigh, looking pained. "What?"

"I wish you'd stop calling me that."

My father, the self-proclaimed *Greatest Djinn alive*, was pouting. I said, "Maybe someday. How about for right now I just don't call you anything." I turned away to leave him to his funk. I was not feeling terribly sympathetic right now.

I made an about face, though, when I thought of all the years of misunderstanding, stubbornness, misinformation, and where that had gotten us. "I'm glad you came back. Dylan was right. I never believed you were dead, which just made it worse because it felt like a betrayal. Like you didn't care." He sighed, the bushy red eyebrows crashing in a fierce frown, his mouth set in a grimace. "You meant well, you and Phoebe both." He glared.

"Mother," I corrected. "My boots...that day—was that really her I trudged around on all over school and the playground?"

"Yes, Tempest, but you remember it incorrectly. It was not your first day of school. It was the first day... your mother wasn't supposed to be around you, after our—"

"Diversion?"

He nodded and his expression was lit with tenderness...

for me, and I realized, for my mother. "You still love her." I couldn't help it. My surprise was genuine.

A shocked look met mine as his head came up and his voice bounced off the walls. "Of course I love her. She's been my mate for a very, very, *very* long time. I'm sorry this was so hard on you, my sweet girl, but you and River will live to see that nineteen years is but a wisp in the life of Paramortals like us." His expression held so much love as he stood there that the years between us fell away.

Closing my eyes I reached for the same man who'd played with me and River and mother on the lawn that day when I was seven. I sighed as his mighty arms embraced me. "I love you, Du—I love you, papa."

I felt the rate of his heart increase when he sighed and held me for the briefest of moments. He cleared his throat and held me at arms length. "Tempest. Please understand. I would stay if I could. Everything I've done, everything your mother and Dylan and the rest of our people did, was to keep you safe until you traveled the path to change."

I was seeing him differently, and already feeling the loss. My throat clogged. When he wiped my cheeks with his thumbs, they came away with the residue of sooty tears. I'd just been reunited with him after most of my life without him. "Why must you go?"

"I have to take River away to heal. If he stays here the damage that witch started will continue. And we can't afford to be vulnerable during the Chaos." He hugged me tighter and leaned down to rub his cheek across my hair. "Have I told you what a spectacular molten storm you were today?"

I pushed back from him, eyes wide. "Where did *that* come from? That wasn't just air and water."

"No," his big grin was full of pride. "I believe you got a bit of your ol' man's Djinni genes, baby. You smoked it."

I stepped back as I heard Dylan's SUV drive away. "Can I contact you?"

"If you absolutely must, but it has to be a matter of dire need. The *Aretuu* will still be looking for us all. When your mother returns... tell her I love her." His eyes narrowed with pain, and I knew it was because he wouldn't be here to tell her himself after so long. "We'll be back."

Jack entered as Dutch turned away.

"Papa—"

My father cradled my unconscious brother in his arms like a baby. "We're out of time, Tempest. Take care of her, Lang," his voice boomed. Jack took my hand and pulled me away as mist filled the room and Dutch's body expanded, muscles bulging, his entire form becoming transparent. I saw the night sky through the walls. He was really leaving.

"But when—" I called out to him.

My father's form had begun to fade, but the deep echo of his words hung in the room long after he and my brother disappeared into the fog-like air. "When you need us the most." To anyone else's ears it would have sounded like the barest hint of a breeze.

"But you just came back," I sighed.

CHAPTER 19

TEMPE

Sat 7am Danger in Paradise?

THE CRISIS WAS over and I could relax. Exhaustion weighed my limbs down as I drooped bonelessly across the lounge chair. I'd barely had time to sleep the last two weeks. Last night all I'd done was rerun my meager time with Dutch, imprinting it on my memory in case it was another twenty years before I saw him again. *Zeus*, I hoped not.

Today was a new day. I didn't have to work, and I had a date to the Grand Ball! My squeal of happiness briefly shut off the sounds of the morning. It was like a *real* fairytale, as in make-believe, not like the faerie sitting next to me. At dawn I'd found Arabella on my windowsill, tapping against it to wake me up.

Armed with two cups of coffee, I walked with her toward the Forge, her long legs keeping pace with mine with halting heron-like grace—*pause, glide… pause, glide…*

Now, her feathers caught the sunrise, brightening into corals and reds as she flew over the water, extending her wings toward me and making a graceful two-footed landing. During our morning "talks" Bella often didn't change out of her stunning feathered plumage, choosing instead to simply absorb the idyllic beauty of my bayou.

That's an exaggeration. The Forge belonged to no one. The fact that Harmony was bordered on two sides by the power laden swamp and on another by the fairgrounds was just luck. Or fate. It was beautiful though, and practically speaking, it was all mine to enjoy… *paradise*, except when there were activities on the fairgrounds.

So, on Saturday mornings, Bella would visit and clear her head from the pressures of running the Faerie Inn; and with Petre, the vast Bright Fae empire.

I leaned back in one of the plastic Adirondack chairs I'd picked up at Wal-Mart. They lasted longer than cypress in our humid environment. "Are you sure you don't want to sit?"

Standing in the low chair Bella's bird face was level with mine. She blinked and looked back at the water. I took that as a no. "I'm sorry about all the damage I did to the Inn the other day. I hope you were able to fix it fairly easily."

Another blink.

"Good."

She nipped at mosquitoes buzzing around my head while I watched the bayou come to life, the sounds and sights of serenity. A turtle popped his head up for air and shad shimmered along the top of the water sparkling white in the sun-risen light. A single mourning dove called from a tall cypress.

Gradually, as the light of the sun brightened the sally grass and reeds along the edge of the bayou and life awakened below, the surface rippled, the rising mist revealing a perfect Monet reproduction in sunrise golds, pinks, and blues. If only I could have captured the sounds, the sharp throaty chatter of the squirrel, the answering cry of the mother sparrow protecting her nest.

I enjoyed watching tiny water bugs as they made elegant trails on the surface of the water, the infrequent attack of a small fish disrupting their patterns. As the sun lifted over the tree branches, the breeze moved patches of mist along the surface. Spanish moss waved its ancient lace and cypress fronds drifted down from above.

At the edge of my peripheral vision a snake slid silently by the line of cypress knees that looked like a band of druids in the dim light. Near there, a minnow jumped creating a flurry of overlapping concentric circles.

Bella strode stealthily through the shallow water toward the minnows in search of her morning meal. She jumped at a sudden *caw* and the distant cacophony, spreading her wings and lifting into the air to survey the threat.

All sound ceased but resumed its delicate song within seconds. Bella swooped down quickly taking advantage of the brief lull to snatch her breakfast from the water, and then landed by my chair once again.

"I couldn't sleep," I said. "I keep wondering where Phoebe is, and if River's okay, and wishing I'd had a little more time with Dutch. I know. It's selfish." I'd walked the large high-ceilinged rooms of my house, the lonely silence driving me outside as soon as my eyes opened.

Bella extended her glorious wings resting one tip lightly on my shoulder for comfort. I smiled into her steady lavender gaze. "Thanks."

Thirty yards from the large cypress an alligator slid quietly into the water after its prey, sinking just below the surface, her tiny offspring clinging to her back. I smiled at the familiar sight, scratching Bella's downy crown.

In the space of a heartbeat, as if some ecological breaker box controlled the swamp, a switch flipped and all sound and movement *ceased*, the air becoming thick and dank.

Staring into the mist, every nerve and feather rigid, Bella studied the threat with her more powerful fae senses and shivered, her feathers fluttering like a wave from head to tail.

"What is it, Bella?" I whispered.

The entire natural realm sensed a hostile disquiet like a ghost walking over its grave but with the flip of that astral switch, the primitive system reset and the threat moved on. I read Bella's silent message, *for now*. She transformed and plopped down in the other chair, sighing. "Tempe, these are the most uncomfortable chairs. I'm going to send over a couple made by one of our guests. They never rot."

I chuckled, but she wasn't finished. "Why don't you get Dylan to check *that* out?" She pointed a long gold fingernail toward the water. "It's something that doesn't belong here."

We sat watching for another twenty minutes but when nothing happened, she flew off to the Inn, and I went inside to get dressed and go to town.

Jack

8am "A tattoo doesn't belong on that body, young lady."

Ryan called to ask me how to fill out the final paperwork on the Nuck—Meeker's murder and River's disappearance. There wasn't much fudging to do since we could easily blame the murder, theft and kidnapping all on Will Crain, who wasn't around to dispute the charges. Jordie fed a leak to Melissa about River taking his mother on a cruise to Alaska. Melissa faithfully reported it to her mother and surprise! It made the morning *Tribune*.

"So are you going to tell me what really went on in that camp?" Ryan asked.

"If I told you—"

"Yeah, I've heard that one—"

"You'd probably run screaming into the night, never to return."

There was silence on the other end for several seconds. "Considering the source, maybe I should leave now."

I took a deep breath and rubbed my eyes, which seemed to have a pound of grit between them. I didn't want to lose Ryan, but if he was inclined to leave, now would be better while his view of the world only included terrorists and serial killer bad guys. "You know I wouldn't try to stop you if you wanted to leave."

"You're serious." After a pause, Ryan spoke. "Sorry, Jack. You're not getting rid of me that easily. I've been your wingman for nearly half my life. If I wanted predictable, I would have been a grocery store manager like my dad."

He heard my relieved sigh through the phone and chuckled. "Was that a test, Laser?" he asked.

"No, Ryan, that was for real," I said, all humor erased from my voice. "Just... don't wait forever to change your mind. You may find yourself enlightened about things you'd be healthier and happier not knowing."

"That was cryptic."

"Just remember what I said, and Ryan... I'm glad you have my six."

"Roger that."

I hung up and went looking for Jordie. "Jordie, if you have to work today, you'd better get a move on," I yelled down the hallway.

She made a dash from the bathroom to her bedroom and something caught my eye. I stalked down the hall and pounded on her door.

"What have you done?" I called through the closed door, my voice sharp.

"Wha—" Jordie opened the door in her underwear and sleep tunic.

I pushed into her bedroom. "Let me see your hip, Jordie."

"What is it?"

I pointed at her thigh, "That. What is *that?*" I asked in a strangled voice.

Jordie looked down at her leg and blanched. "I... Daddy?" Her expression was all innocence and confusion but I wasn't buying it. I saw guilt and pleading. "When did you get a tattoo?" I stood in the open door with my arms crossed. "A tattoo doesn't belong on that body, young lady."

"I-I didn't." Tears filled her voice and her eyes were wide, "Daddy, I didn't."

"Well, then what the f…" I closed my eyes willing myself to chill, and that chilly expression was what she saw when I looked at her again. "Explain that thing on your thigh that looks very much like a tattoo."

She blinked and tears streamed down her cheeks. Looking at it again she gasped, "I c-can't. It wasn't there last night."

That stopped me. I thought about the last few days, the many surprises. I couldn't vouch for whether the mark—it wasn't as distinct as a tattoo—had been there the day before or not.

"Please, Daddy, believe me." She wrapped her arms around my stiff torso, her words muffled into my shirt, "I don't even like tattoos."

My arms encircled her automatically. It was true. The musicians and actors displayed on her walls sported more blank skin than most. She'd always been against "inking up" as she called it. I set my chin on top of her head, relief and concern, weighing in proportionately. "Okay, baby, we're okay. We'll figure it out later. Go get ready for work; it's late."

I didn't know yet what the mark on Jordie's thigh meant, but I reminded myself a good investigator wouldn't find her guilty before the facts were all in.

Jordie was subdued on the way to Aurora Borealis. I reminded her that her grandparents would pick her up after work since—

"You're taking Cinderella to the ball." She actually clapped her hands in delight. "I'm glad I'll get to see her in that gown at least."

I smiled. I was looking forward to it as well. "I hope it fits."

"Oh, I'm sure it will. Tempe's going to look awesome. Aurora said she's never been to a dance before in her life."

That had shocked me. I vowed to make it a memorable night for her because... I was falling for the woman, despite her 'quirks', and somebody needed to show her there was more beneath the surface than a delivery person and a storm witch, and more to look forward to than her responsibilities. Being responsible was honor-able but you could get caught in that trap and never experience everything life could offer.

I looked over at my daughter. I guess that observation could apply to me as well.

"I love you, baby."

She smiled, and this time it reached her eyes. "You're just a big softie, ya know."

"Yeah, that's what you'll think if you really come home with a tattoo, young lady." I frowned. "Be sure to ask your boss and Tempe about that rash. Maybe Ms. Aurora has a cream or something for it."

CHAPTER 20

TEMPE

9:15 am Hell to pay…

AURORA CALLED AT NINE. "Are you coming by to get your dress?"

"I'll be there shortly. Bella just left and I was straightening up around here a bit." Who knew, I might get lucky and bring a certain ex-Navy jock home with me tonight. "I'm not sure how I feel about Jack buying me a dress."

"Well, don't think about it then. I dare say, when you see it, that won't be a problem." She hung up before I could disagree.

I slipped on some jeans and a t-shirt and walked out to my truck. I could see myself in an evening gown in my ratty old mail truck. Surely I wouldn't be driving myself to the ball *or* driving myself home.

I didn't have enough experience at this. *Hello?* Like none.

I made a stop at the fairgrounds to find out what I had to do to get Marty registered for the wiener race. They told me I had until Monday to bring him by the booth and get his temporary collar, racing number and pay the entry fee. I'd have to remind him that I entered a black and tan so he didn't show up as that scruffy gray mixed mutt version I saw him in the other night.

They were working on the course. Volunteers sat amid sheets of plywood and boards, creating a dozen or more long narrow doghouses which would act as starting gates. At the other end of the course workmen were drawing the finish line and marking it with bright pink tape. I overheard one woman talking to her friend about how she planned to get her dog to cross the line first. She apparently had a female in heat and planned to hold her at the other end so her male would have "incentive" to *finish strong*.

I had no idea a dog race could engender such ferocity, but I was sure there would be more than just her dog hotfooting it to that corner of the end zone. Which just might work in Marty's favor.

AURORA AND JORDIE were busy changing out a window

in the front of the shop when I got there. "Hey, divas! Getting rid of the Mardi Gras colors?"

"Hi, Tempe," Jordie called. "We're putting the last minute 'arrivals' for Mardi Gras in that window and the new Spring fashions in this one." She beamed, proud of her new vernacular.

Aurora pointed to a purse on the floor behind Jordie. "Jordie, why don't you try your hand at this window and I'll get Tempe fixed up."

"You mean, by myself?" Jordie fist pumped a silent *yes*.

"Totally. Let's see what you come up with. When you're done I'll critique it, and we'll put the finishing touches on it." She eased the beaded room divider aside for me and called over her shoulder, "Yell if you need anything."

I accepted a cup of tea from her—store bought Mango Jasmine—and we sat at the little iron table in the other room watching Jordie sort through the purses, dresses, shoes and jewelry building her strategy for the window.

"I'm so glad you suggested I hire that teenager." Aurora watched Jordie thoughtfully for a moment before turning to me. "Are you ready to see your dress?"

I nodded.

She pointed to a dress bag hanging on the wall and a tray of accessories nearby. "Let's do it."

Aurora was right. The dress was beyond beautiful. I tried to see myself through Jack's eyes. What had he said? He'd like to see me all dressed up. He'd chosen a dress of storm cloud blue crinoline or... "What do you call this stuff?" I raised the fabric of the skirt carefully.

"It's tulle. I'll give you the runway spiel. 'Eye catching stonework of silver, aquamarine, and rainbow hues decorate the strapless sweetheart neckline and torso of this lovely designer creation. The slender waistline drips with ribbons of silver and smoke colored lace embedded with more crystals. Embroidered flowers, rhinestones and beads cover the soft ombre layers of tulle that overlay a flesh toned skirt of lace covered satin'."

I stared at myself in the mirror as Aurora murmured for me to, "Lift my feet... turn this way." She placed long Swarkovsky earrings in my ears and brushed my hair. "I'd use a curling iron but I don't want to risk getting heat near that skirt."

Her voice was just noise. I was mesmerized by the vision of the woman in the three-way mirror. She tilted her head and studied me. I was alien to her as well. "I don't deserve this."

Aurora exploded, and I thought she was going to throw the brush. "Tempest Pomeroy. Where did that come from?"

"I—it's not me. I can't be her." My heart was pounding, and I turned, intending to slip out of the dress and don my familiar jeans, but Jack stood in the doorway. Aurora walked out of the room pulling the curtain across the opening.

I looked down at the dress, my hands grasping the skirt to have something to do.

"Turn around and look in the mirror," he said quietly.

I did, careful not to catch the heel of my shoe in the skirt. When I looked up he was behind the woman, his eyes burning, like hot ice or the palest silver fog. "I've never seen anything so beautiful." His voice was deep, hoarse. He drew his hands down the sides of *her* dress barely touching it, as if *she* were a precious treasure. "I can't stop looking at you."

It was a dream, a story, and I was the heroine... "No, this isn't real. Jack, I'm not this..." My insides churned; doubt, anticipation and fear warring inside me. I wanted this more than I'd wanted anything *ever*, but I couldn't envision it, couldn't mesh the *me* I knew with this woman staring back at me. She looked like Tempe but different. *Beautiful.* I should use the confidence her image gave me, but I was afraid, afraid there'd be hell to pay. Wasn't it safer *not* to dream?

"I don't know, Jack."

"I feel your skin under my hands. You're real. I knew you'd look awesome in that dress. This is the you I see every day; just in different clothing. Tonight, I'll look different, too, but I'll still be the man who wants you."

I watched him lean toward *her*. Felt him kiss *my* neck.

"And I still want to peel all that glitter and lace off inch…" kiss… "by"…kiss… "inch."

I wasn't looking at *her* any longer, but the tall sexy man beside her. I wished it were already midnight and the ordeal… "Can we skip the ball, and go straight to—uh…"

He chuckled and his breath warmed my skin. "Nope, because I want to enjoy watching other people watch you, and *hate* that you're with me, not them. If you find yourself wanting to run away…" he lifted an ornate silver and crystal mask from the box at his feet and handed it to me by the stem.

I held it up to my face. It was elegant and with it masking my discomfort, I felt an immediate sense of relief, and maybe… a bit of daring.

"It helps, doesn't it?" He grinned at me over my shoulder. "Take care of that dress. I'll be by to pick you up at seven."

He stopped short of the door and turned. "I almost forgot. Did Jordie show you and Aurora that rash on her thigh?"

I shook my head. "She might have shown Aurora but she's busy with customers. I'll check it out myself and let you know tonight. Would that be okay?"

"That'll work." He gave me another once-over, a thumbs-up, and left smiling. Which put me in a pretty happy mood as well. Tonight was going to *so unreal.*

~

Tempe

7 pm Hop in, Cinderella before your coach turns into a pumpkin.

AT five MINUTES 'til seven I was still fiddling with the skirt of my dress to keep it from dragging the ground, making sure I didn't snag it on the heel of shoes that were entirely too high, and worrying with my hair.

The doorbell rang.

I inhaled deeply, eased it out and opened the door, stepping back out of the way.

The man standing on my doorstep bowed, the shiny black of his formal suit reflecting moonlight. He was tall and broad but I didn't recognize him until he spoke. "Madam, your coach has arrived."

"Hello, Ryan."

He smiled.

"Where's Jack?" I asked attempting to look around him but he blocked my view.

"He's waiting. Are you ready?"

I grabbed my rhinestone clutch. "I'll take that for you," he said and lifted my purse from my fingertips.

As I stepped onto the veranda, the bright moonlight illuminated a mile long silver limo on the street. Ryan laughed at my gawking expression.

"It wouldn't fit in the driveway."

"I guess not." Ryan took a firm grip on my other hand and placed it around his elbow, as I descended the few steps to the front walk. Then he escorted me to a spot near the street.

I understood why, when the door in the center slid smoothly out and up like a wing. "It's called a jet door," Ryan said, grinning. "Kind of appropriate, huh?"

But I wasn't listening. I was watching Jack as he exited through the jet door. Dressed in his white Navy tails and black pants he looked like a model for a Navy recruitment video. "You're gorgeous, Jack." I ran a finger over his white bow tie, rolled the smooth pearl buttons between my fingertips, and lifted one hand to take a closer look at his cuff links.

I angled my eyes up to him seductively. "My hero," I said. I felt a new sense of power, not the magical kind, but a sense of confidence in myself and... I nearly smiled when I figured it out. The Tempestaerie wasn't the only being that had quickened during the last few weeks. Tempest, the woman, was coming of age. And tonight at least, she was beautiful, and alluring, and dare I say, sexy. I did smile then, and Jack seemed to read my mind.

Ryan coughed, "I'll just take my seat behind the wheel.

Jack watched Ryan run around the front of the car then his smiled kicked up slyly. "You embarrassed my wingman."

"I doubt it." I pointed toward the car. "I wasn't expecting this, Jack."

"That makes it all the more satisfying for me."

"I don't know, I'm not really built for this," I said, looking down.

"Oh, yeah, Sweetheart. Believe me, you're built for it." He winked and I slapped my gloves against his shoulder.

"Aren't you cold?" He ran his hands up and down my arms, a sweet gesture which was totally unnecessary.

"You're forgetting to whom you're speaking."

"Nope." I got a glimpse of sea-foam green eyes and feathered laugh lines just before he kissed me. A warm casual kiss at first, I felt its magic surging through my veins like warm water shoving ice floes out of the way during a spring thaw. My toes curled in the tight spiky heels. The ice floes were melting fast and I felt desire like never before. The scent of his warm hard body enticed me. At the very least I wanted to crawl into his bed tonight, let him show me the stratosphere again and stay there until morning.

"You two could *get down* right here, I won't tell a soul, but it would be a waste of a limo, and a driver, and that rockin' dress."

Jack stepped back and grinned, "He has a point."

I wiped the little smear of lipstick off his lower lip and smiled back. "I agree." Jack's eyebrows rose, his eyes crinkling.

Ryan placed one hand on the jet door. "Hop in, then Cinderella. It'll be pumpkin time before you know it."

I didn't care for the fairytale history of pumpkins and balls so I ignored him, choosing instead to look at the evening as new possibilities, a new reality. One didn't have to live in a fairytale to be happy. I could see a glimpse of it from here, standing in front of Harmony with this man.

CHAPTER 21

TEMPE

1-900-Psycho

I FELT EYES ON ME, lots of them, but figured it was because everyone who came through the door was announced, *and* I was on the arm of a physically imposing Jack Lang, who was a head taller than everyone else. In his Navy dress uniform he oozed sex appeal without even trying.

With the mask hiding my face, it was easier to display a cool facade, *any* facade, I couldn't usually pull that off. Mark one up for masks.

Jack chuckled beside me. "Don't get used to that thing. You'll have to take it off eventually. The suspension of the law only applies to the hours before the Court is revealed and Fat Tuesday."

"What law?"

"There's a law against concealing your face with a mask. But it's suspended on Fat Tuesday and unofficially waved during the Grand Ball."

"Oh."

"Hey." Montana strode up next to me, her face half covered with a mask of deep blue feathers and gems. Warrior types never sidle, slouch or stroll. She looked me over and shook her head. "Jack, how the hell did you get her into a dress? Don't bristle, Temp, you look amazing."

My charming date said, "I could say the same about you, Montana. That's a stunning costume. What are you, anyway?"

Montana's long blue-black hair was braided with ribbons and piled loosely on her head with a comb. The woman who cared little for "female trappings" had turned into a seductress. Her dress had a deep royal fitted bodice with spaghetti straps that draped off her shoulders, exposing the circular symbol under the skin of her shoulder blade, and dove to a point below her waist. The skirt's long feather-light layers danced with each move.

Her eyes flared, turning a brilliant cobalt, and her smile

was sly when she answered, looking at Jack. "Why, a Dinnshencha, of course."

I laughed.

Jack's mouth quirked, "You make a good one. Whatever that is."

Montana laughed. "One of these days, Jack..." She turned back to me, "Tempe, you'd better hang close. I've seen some hungry female predators locked on the handsome Commander." Jack went off to get us a drink and I asked Montana if she'd seen Aurora.

"She's over there. Sitting next to Jane."

Across the room, dressed in the gaudiest multicolored outfit I'd ever seen, was Jane. It was styled strictly to grab attention. "That getup came straight out of the circus."

Aurora sat at the other end, plain midnight cloth stretched over the table. She was dressed in her usual understated elegance. For tonight's ball it was a shimmering pearlescent shift, two matching crystals dangling from her ears to touch her shoulder blades, her long black and silver hair loose and flowing, and only the amulet as decoration. The contrast between the two "fortune tellers" couldn't have been more stark.

Aurora sent me a smile, the corner of her mouth turned up as if to say, *I can't believe I'm doing this.* We knew that if not for a great cause, one near and dear to Montana's heart, she wouldn't have been caught dead this close to Jane Fortune. To her left in front of a backdrop of glittering stars, crescent moons and smilie suns was Jane, all two hundred and thirty pounds squished into a five-foot frame.

Jane's dark hair was covered in a purple velvet and gold paisley turban and she'd pasted a green stone in the center of her forehead. She'd used eyeliner from her bottom lids nearly to her eyebrows making her eyes appear to be empty black holes. Her caftan was cheap purple taffeta and Jane had pulled the crisscrossed ties until the fleshy mounds of her chest threatened to tear the fabric. She was armed with all of her standard psychic paraphernalia—oversized tarot cards, a tray of candles, and a green "gazing ball" identical to one I'd seen in the garden section at Wal-Mart.

Her throat, ears and fingers were adorned with so much jewelry it was a wonder she could sit upright. Besides her name, two other obvious "tells" spoke of her charlatan status—the most visible, the line of mismatched fan bulbs encircling the poster of sun, moon and stars on the panel behind her. And most telling, the tiny red flame flickering from within the gazing ball, in the silhouette of a Christmas candle, complete with an electric cord that ran from the ball to the wall.

Yeah. *Very mystical.*

I looked down at the nameplate in front of Jane. "Look." I pointed to the label. Montana snickered.

Jane's hand-printed card read: *Have your Fortune told by a real Psycho.*

Tempe

"Mother of all the Gods, who is that!"

AFTER I STOPPED LAUGHING I asked, "Has anyone asked Jane for a reading?"

Montana looked irritated. "Only flower man."

I swiveled toward her. "Dickhead?"

"Mm-hmm. They are an item."

"Eeuw!" I said. "On second thought... maybe that works. What about Aurora?"

"She's bringing in the cheese for the shelter," Montana said. "This is the first break she's had. Jane keeps trying to get Montana's customers to give her a try but so far, no takers. I think they only take her card to keep from being seen standing near her for too long."

"It's a lovely costume," I teased.

"If you care for overweight charlatan floozies. You'd think she worked for 1-900–Sex instead of 1-900–Psycho," Montana said. "Maybe when the circus comes through this summer, they'll take her with them."

"I know one sheriff that would be happy to see her go," I said.

A deep voice over my shoulder said, "I hope I'm the only sheriff you're familiar with that *intimately*. Whose behind would he be happy to see on their way out of town?"

The inflection he put on the word "intimately" made me warm in the most private places, and I lost my train of thought. The promise of becoming his lover tonight hung in the wind and *menori* shivered her reaction.

Montana bumped me back to the present laughing, and said to Jack, "Ms. Gaudy Fortune."

Jack said, "True sometimes... and yet she has her uses. I would never have known about your mother's 'protectors' if it hadn't been for Jane, not that quickly."

Montana said, "Why don't you go donate to the cause?"

"With Jane?" I raised my eyebrows and waited for her to snicker, but she said seriously, "No, fool. With Aurora. Get *real* value for your contribution."

"Hmm. I don't know if I can stand to hear any more predictions about my future right now." I looked at Jack, who gave me a crooked grin. "I have my own ideas of what's going to happen in my immediate future."

Jack's eyes flared with heat. *Good*. He had the same idea. Hadn't he said when he saw me in this dress the first time he wanted to peel it off one layer at a time? I'd intentionally added a few layers this evening, just in case, which had taken some creativity the way this gown was made.

"Be brave, sweetheart. We weathered the storms," he winked, "of the last two weeks. What could be worse?"

"Clever play on words, Jack," Montana said as our gazes met, hers with that sharp angled brow. It didn't take a mindlink to understand her thoughts—*he doesn't know about Chaos?* I caught myself before I answered aloud. I returned a look that meant, *Please don't open that can of worms tonight.*

"I guess I can do it for your cause."

"What is the charity?" Jack asked.

I turned to him. "Oh, I figured you knew being in law enforcement."

Montana interrupted. "You can blame that one on me. I'm very protective of my people."

Jack scratched his head, "Your people? Is that, like, different than Paramortals?" His voice sounded dubious.

"I'm—how would you put this?—the director, CEO, COO etc., etc. of a battered women's shelter. My 'people' are the female victims of abuse. I personally respond and 'tend to' any instances of neglect, violence or need for my women and their children. I neither need nor want law enforcement… interference."

Jack bristled. "I think we're going to have to have a meeting or something—"

"I will... now that I know you... fill you in on the shelter's mission and maybe it's whereabouts..." She looked at me, then back at Jack, "Soon." I suspected she meant after the Chaos. After that, it could be a moot point. Things might be radically different in Destiny. I didn't know how, but it could certainly be missing some citizens and minus a sheriff.

Jack opened his mouth to say something and changed his mind, his demeanor relaxing as if realizing where we were once again. "All right. Let's table this discussion for another time. You're not breaking any laws are you?"

Montana stood a little straighter, her features becoming sharper, her eyes going cobalt again. She wouldn't change right here would she? Jack's eyes narrowed, but he stood his ground. "I protect women and children from predators, abusers, those who would harm them. I don't hunt them down, as a rule, unless there are no other options."

They stood eye to eye in a battle of wills, Montana seeming larger and taller than Jack momentarily. I wondered if that was some kind of trick like a glamour or if it was part of her nature, one that threw up a flag of warning to back off before the threat could be born. I knew Montana was not one to back down once she was in protective mode, but this was different—I hoped.

I was right. In a blink she seemed two inches shorter than Jack and looking up at him, she said easily, "I'll give you some local references you can check out, Jack."

Smiling at me she asked, "Tempe, are you going to go see Aurora, or not?"

Jack tilted his head and nodded. "I'll go get us a refill. Still soda?" he asked me. I nodded. "What about you, Montana?"

"I'm fine, thanks. Come on, Temp." She grabbed me by the arm and marched the five or six steps to Aurora's end of the table.

"Tempe, Montana, you know Jane, I presume." Aurora graciously included the other woman in her greeting.

Montana spoke first, "I want to thank you, Jane. I appreciate you offering your, er, expertise for the charity."

"I'm always happy to give back, especially for a food bank, Montana." I hiked my brows over Jane's shoulder at my friend. *Good thinking.* Jane looked toward the crowd, "Oh, it looks like I've got a live one." She lowered those black painted eyes to the ball and slid her hand down to the front of the globe, passing it over its inner light as if divining some celestial wisdom. "Please have a seat. How can the Sultress of Fortune help you, my dear? Palm reading, cards, your navel chart?"

The Sultress of Fortune. When a portly little man seated himself in front of Jane, Montana and I shifted to Aurora's end of the table. "Food bank?" I whispered.

"Six letters—G-O-S-S-I-P. Wonder if he's going to let her look at his navel?"

All three of us chuckled. "Aurora, Montana talked me into letting you do a..."

"An astral seeding?" Aurora asked. "Lovely. Have a seat, Tempe." Montana stood, taking in the growing crowd and making sure Jane wasn't listening in on our conversation.

Aurora took a large shallow shell from her lap and a flask of clear liquid. Pouring about half an inch into the shell, she removed one of her earrings and held it suspended above the surface. Light reflected through its facets sending sparkles across the water but oddly they didn't extend to the table or any of our surroundings. The lights were contained within the bowl.

"You might be interested as well, Montana..." Imitating an actress with a Transylvanian accent, she said, "You vill meet a dahk, dangerrous sstrangah..."

Montana and I laughed. Aurora merely shrugged. "That was freebie. Here's another one for you. It looks like the Chaos is going to hit by Monday. You should remind the good sheriff, Tempe. He'll need some warning to prepare."

I nodded. "You can't get any closer than that?" I dreaded that conversation, but she was right. I'd have to figure out how to fit that explanation in between the ball and our *other* plans.

"I wish I could. This isn't meteorology where each time we learn to forecast it better. As far as I can tell Cache's orbit simply can't be predicted... anticipated, guessed at… but not predicted with any accuracy. And now, for you." She reached across the table and snatched some hair from my scalp.

"Ow!" I complained as she draped the teal and coppery strands across the bowl allowing it to touch the water. She tilted her head as the light flickered across it.

"You will encounter evil… trouble from your lover's past." She frowned. "I'm not clear on the details unfortunately, Tempe. I think the coincidence is messing with my readings."

"Obviously," said Montana remembering Aurora's earlier jest.

Why would I care about trouble from Dylan's past? Unless, it had something to dc with Phoebe. I remembered what Marty'd said, that he knew why Dylan and Dutch had looked at each other the way they had at the Forge before the attempted mindlink.

Aurora shrugged. "I'd better go back to reading palms. Thank you, Jack," she said as Jack arrived and set three glasses of wine down on the table and handed me a soda. I'd decided after the trouble the small amounts of alcohol had caused me I would nix it from my drink list. Last night had been an added case in point. One glass of wine with Kat and I'd gone to bed, not budging until daylight.

"The court is about to be presented," Aurora said. She looked back at the entrance. "They don't even announce the identity of the king until the parade but I can usually figure it out—"

The chatter around us quieted suddenly. Montana and Jack looked over my shoulder.

Montana hissed behind me, a sound I'd never heard from her. "Mother of all the gods! Who is *that*?"

CHAPTER 22

*T*EMPE

"Where'd he get those damn swords?"

WE TURNED as the elder at the door called out, "Conor de Sept Flambé, Knight of his Majesty's realm."

Jack stiffened and muttered, "Which Majesty?"

"What realm?" I wondered aloud.

"Where'd he get those damn swords?" breathed Montana behind me. Leave it to a warrior goddess to appreciate and hone in on the most obvious feature of the newcomer's costume.

The—it seemed lacking somehow to call him a man, though he appeared to be, but I could see why both of them had reacted to the stranger.

He wore a beautiful black and red mask, which was slightly reptilian in design, strapped around his shoulder length black hair. He was shirtless and radiated danger. There were intricate red and black tattoos that resembled bat wings across his shoulders and triceps. He didn't need a costume t-shirt with abs painted on it. The ridges of his torso were well defined and indicated strength and discipline. Matching leather strips banded his bulging biceps and matched the jagged hemmed samurai pants floating about his muscular calves.

"Looks like someone left their video game on too long," said Jack.

The Knight Flambé did indeed look like he'd walked straight from the Samurai Assassin video game into the Grand Ball. His boots were exquisitely tooled silver and bronze, with a belt of the same metals, which glimmered flat against his lower abdomen. When he turned to hand his invitation to the elder there was a collective murmur, and Jack made a low guttural sound.

Two long deadly looking gold and silver swords crisscrossed his back and seemed to shoot fire with each movement down their jagged twisting length. As he listened to the announcement, the knight's hands, girded at the wrist in pewter, bronze and gold to the elbows, fisted and relaxed, making the tendons flex from elbow to chest. *Whew!*

Montana stood like a statue of a Valkyrie, her hands clenching and unclenching, piercing cobalt eyes locked on the figure dressed in precious metals, leather and a lot of bronzed skin. *Menori* reacted restlessly to the dark knight.

So did Jack. It was as if they were meeting as equals on some arena of war—not as I'd described him and Dylan —like dogs fighting over their Poodle. *This* was something elemental, as if they knew each other at their core. It lasted mere seconds but it was as if time during those few seconds amplified, expanded to push away all other sounds and only those of us who *saw, felt, and understood,* well, I didn't understand except to know that something of impetus had passed between them.

Party sounds filtered in again from the other room and the Knight Flambé took three deliberate steps off the platform, glancing toward Montana and away. His sharp predatory gaze met each attendee briefly, and each person acknowledged his presence, like he was studying them one by one and simultaneously erasing himself from their minds. I shook my head. We'd had our share of supernaturals, but this powerful looking soldier, the sexy sword-wielding samurai warrior... was a first.

The newcomer bowed and walked deliberately through the crowd, which parted like the Red Sea to give him and his swords an unencumbered path to the bar. Montana devoured him with her eyes. She had not moved since he walked in the door. Interesting.

"Reckon that's a costume? Or is he some kind of knight in shining armor?" I asked.

Jack said, "He doesn't seem the type." Turning to me he asked, "Does he seem like a good POP to you? Can you tell that kind of thing?"

I shook my head. "We'll have to see if Aurora—oh!" I snapped my fingers and spun around meeting Montana's eyes, hair rising on my neck when I remembered Aurora's earlier words to her. *You will meet a dark, dangerous stranger.* This knight surely qualified.

If she'd been right about Montana what did her words hold for me? My thoughts strayed to Dylan. "Have you seen Dylan around since yesterday?" I asked Jack.

"No, why? Do you think he might know something about this... Flambé character?"

Oh, right. "Er, exactly what I was thinking," I said quickly.

Jack's eyebrow rose. He wasn't buying it. His eyes widened, and he grinned, nodding toward the door, "Isn't that the old man you saved..."

I followed his eyes. It was! Mr. Jackson had just gimped his hunched-over self through the front door. He'd stopped, turning back, just as Elder Rawlins was about to announce him. "The morning we met." I smiled at Jack. "That's him. I wonder what he's waiting for—*Zeus' greasy toupee.*" I couldn't believe my eyes.

Mr. Jackson motioned for his date to hurry, holding his arm out to a small bent-over rosy-cheeked Inez Messer. "Mr. Phineas Jackson, and his lady, Inez Messer."

"Close your mouth, sweetie," came Montana's voice behind me.

I was *totally* at a loss for words. What was going on around here? *Dickhead and Jane Fortune.* "Inez and Mr. Jackson? Maybe the moons *are* colliding," I said to Montana, looking over at Jack. He just shook his head.

She laughed. "Hey, maybe she'll mellow the old bird."

As soon as Inez saw me, she tugged on Mr. Jackson's arm and *hurried* toward us. It took a while. "Tempe, honey, look who asked me to the ball!" She turned to Mr. Jackson and I met Jack's humorous expression over their heads. Stooped over like they were, they were about half his height.

"Phineas, you know Tempe, don't you?" I cringed, knowing what to expect from Mr. Jackson.

"Nice to see you, Tempest." He glanced at Inez and she nodded at him. He looked back at me and said, "I want to thank you for saving my life." He seemed to get in the spirit of the *thank you* then, adding, "I met my lovely Inez at the hospital. If it hadn't been for you..." he gave me a sweet smile and suddenly he looked younger, well, maybe eighty instead of eighty something.

"I'm glad I was able to help, Mr. Jackson."

"Please, call me Phineas."

Montana mouthed over his head, *Please!*

"Phineas."

He took Jack's offer to escort him to the drink table and Inez turned excitedly, "Isn't he just *bootilicious*, Tempe? Oh, my, I think I'm in love." Her lips quivered as a tear streaked down that pale pink skin. *THE* ring was nowhere in sight.

Inez looked over her shoulder toward the direction Jack and Phineas had taken. "You know I volunteer at the hospital as a candy striper." I didn't think they still called them that but I got her drift.

"Is that where you met Mr—Phineas?" I asked.

The joy was evident in her smile and the way her eyes lit up when she told me, "I think it was love at first sight. You know when I entered his room, his eyes locked on mine and we never looked back. That first night I asked him to the ball, and he said, 'I'd go with you to the moon, if you get me out of here.' Isn't that romantic? Most people would be afraid of space travel, but for me he'd…" she teared up again. "Well, I was glad when he finally got off that morphine and was released so we could actually date. Trying to have normal relations in his hospital room was tricky."

I coughed to cover the laugh that bubbled up. "I'm very happy for you both, Ms. Inez." I was happy for her. It was just… having dealt with Mr. Jackson for so long I wondered if it would last.

I couldn't help but feel encouraged though. Unorthodox relationships could work, and one's mate could truly come out of nowhere.

Jack came over and said, "It's time to introduce the court, and I promised to escort the ladies to the stage."

"Lucky ladies," I said.

"Don't go anywhere. Particularly, don't go delving into the mystery of the swordsman."

"Jealous?" I teased. It felt good to play with him. He'd been smiling more since finding out about Destiny's other side. Who would have thought?

A dimple appeared in his cheek and in front of a full ballroom he leaned down and sealed his lips to mine. We barely touched, but his mouth was hot, his tongue exploring, briefly taking the kiss deeper, making all my thoughts disappear. My concentration was on the taste of his kiss, matching my tongue with his, his big hands on my shoulders as he pulled away. I moaned aloud, I think. "Yeah," he muttered. He planted another brief peck on my lips, the expression on his face fierce when he squinted into my eyes, his voice husky. "I won't be long."

All I could do was nod as he walked away, making his way to the stage. My eyes followed him for a couple heartbeats then I went looking for Montana. It didn't take long to spot her. She was standing at the end of the bar watching the knight like some fan girl, looking like she was desperate to get her hands on either his swords, or him. Or both.

THE NEXT TWO hours were filled with presentations of the court, dancing to Zydeco music, a whiskey tasting, and the costume contest. Someone suggested a yay or nay vote on the 'samurai knight' for first place but he nixed that with hardly a glance. *He could be sheriff of the world with looks like that.*

The band played one of my favorites, "Lovesong" and Jack asked me to dance. It was wonderfully romantic, just to be in his arms. His hand trailed down my shoulder blades and settled in the small of my back. My heart raced. So far the night had been more than I'd dreamed and there were hours left to enjoy.

"Tired?" he asked, looking down at me.

"A little. But it's a good kind of tired since things worked out like they did. I'm enjoying myself more than I expected."

His face was so close I could see the pores in his rugged tan, and the flecks of green in the silver of his eyes. But I eventually settled on his lips, which I desperately wanted on mine, as soon as possible. "Thanks for inviting me, *and*, for the dress. It's not something I would have chosen for myself."

"You're welcome. But I told you it was a selfish gesture. The night isn't over yet. When you've taken in the whole Grand Ball experience, we'll adjourn." His sexy smile slanted to reveal a dimple. "This night is for you. You call the shots." Then the music crescendoed and as the song ended, he dipped me over his arm and kissed me until I thought I'd melt off the end of his fingertips. The applause was probably my imagination.

11:40pm

"Your life is about to get more complicated."

I LOST track of Montana around 10:30. Jack was escorting the ladies of the court to the stage so I went in search of Aurora who had left her end of the divining table and disappeared. I found her in the garden, communing with the garden spirits. "You don't like parties?"

"I don't like being a fifth wheel at these functions, but elder Rawlins is a dear friend, and I promised to do readings for Montana's shelter."

"I have a question for you. Jack said Jordie still had that rash on her leg and he accused her of getting a tattoo. Did she show it to you?"

Aurora nodded. "There's nothing that will fix what ails Jordie."

"Why? What's wrong?" I cast a glance at the door. Aurora's shoulders slumped a bit as she sat down on the concrete bench. Her eyes held a hint of pity. *Uh-oh.*

"I'm afraid your life is about to get more complicated."

Again? I braced myself. "How?"

"The mark on Jordie's thigh is no tattoo, but a prophetic *deremelei* of the Quantus."

I was stunned speechless. "But that means she… she's—"

"—a brand new Paramortal."

"Get out!" I exclaimed. "Jack Lang's daughter is a Paramortal?"

"Interesting development, wouldn't you say?" Aurora watched me as the possibilities and ramifications buzzed through my mind like a band of mosquitoes, none of them lighting for long.

"But how is that possible?" Footsteps sounded on the stone walkway.

"That's the easy answer." Aurora rose, "One or both of her parents is a Paramortal."

"Jack? *Zeus' nebulous newborn!* I can't believe it. Jordie, a Paramortal."

"Paramortal, my ass!"

CHAPTER 23

TEMPE

This is why they call it the pumpkin hour

JACK'S VOICE cracked the night in the quiet garden. He marched up to Aurora, hands on his hips towering over her, eyes blazing in his angry face. Why did he have to find out like this? I watched, aching for him as he whirled back toward the entrance, pressing his fist to his close eyes, then spun back toward Aurora. He looked... terrified.

Of course. As caring and responsible a father as he was, he had to be. He'd only been in this new, *enlightened* place for a couple of days. Before that he'd been determined to find the safest most unadventurous place to raise his "baby girl". This was a blow to say the least.

"Jack, it's not like she's going to turn into a Djinni or... something like me."

"I should hope not."

My heart shrank back, stunned at his words. He stared at me, then his shoulders sagged and he started pacing. "I'm sorry, Tempe. But this Paramortal shit is dangerous, and she's my baby girl, and..." his anguished voice cracked as he looked from me to Aurora. "This has to be a mistake."

He stopped pacing, his eyes concerned. "What can I do? What if we leave here, get away from that... super pulse thing. I could take her anywhere. Just tell me where it's safe."

Aurora sighed, compassion clear on her face. "I'm sorry, my friend. Becoming a Paramortal is a matter of heredity not proximity to leylines."

Jack spun suddenly in a half circle, his leg extended with a *thwack*, as he karate-kicked the trunk of a giant oak tree. "That bitch!" The sight of our sheriff, a respected Navy officer in dress tails, kicking a tree was so incongruous I nearly laughed. "I should have known something weird was wrong with her."

I raised my eyebrows at Aurora. She shrugged as if saying, *now's not the time to bring up the alternative.* If his ex being a bitch because she was a Paramortal was bad, then what did that make me?

He let out a pained sigh, "Isn't there some kind of...s-spell you can do to reverse it? Better yet, send us all back to eight months ago… before I ran for election…"

Hallelujah. He finally—thankfully—shut his mouth.

A long uncomfortable silence ensued while Aurora and I watched Jack struggle with this new threat to his sanity, and his family.

"Tempe," his agonized gaze locked with mine. Poor guy. It was impossible not to feel sorry for him. "Do you mind if we go?"

I smiled, encouragingly, I hoped. "I'm not sure I could stand in these heels much longer anyway." I looked at Aurora. "I'll talk to you tomorrow."

"Good night. And Jack, remember, Jordie is still your teenage daughter." I added, You might consider talking to your parents about this."

Distracted, Jack just nodded and called Ryan on his cell phone. I waved goodbye to Montana as Jack dragged me outside to the waiting limo, where he collapsed against the seat and reached for the open bottle of champagne.

IT WAS a testament to how well Ryan knew his friend that he made no comment when we met him at the curb, *before* midnight. I'd halfway expected a joke or two.

He left the music off in the rear of the limo, though I could hear the hard rock playing in the cab, perhaps chosen out of habit from his years in the Navy, or to give us a buffer so we could discuss *whatever* had gone wrong. But so far Jack had been quiet, his posture military straight in the seat, hands gripping his knees. He stared through the window at passing scenery but I knew he saw none of it.

Ryan stopped at a light when a long stream of revelers who had brought their Mardi Gras party to the downtown streets were slow to cross.

Jack blew out a breath, his head sinking to his chest. I took a chance and placed my hand on his sleeve. He tensed but when I started to remove it, he covered it with his and looked at me. "I'm really sorry, Tempe. I wanted this to be a special night for you."

I tilted my head and smiled at him, "It was one of the best nights of my life, Jack. I mean it. Do you want to talk about it? I know it was a shock."

A short, hard bark escaped him, not one of real mirth. "You could say that." He patted my hand absently, "It's... well, after everything that's happened in the last two days, you'd think nothing could surprise me. I was ready to accept just about anything." His fingers squeezed the bridge of his nose.

"But that was when it was about us people, not your own flesh and blood," I offered.

He sighed, not looking at me, "Yes." His head bounced against the seat back and I felt a wave of tenderness and compassion for him—along with my frustration over his inability to accept *us*.

But the man *had* stepped up. He'd jumped in fearlessly, ignorantly perhaps, but he'd kept going after everything he'd seen until we'd saved River. *And* he'd confronted Paige knowing the strange and inexplicable from the days before might be superseded by something far worse. He'd been right.

I admired him more every day. I wished I could ease some of the fear and stress he was experiencing with a touch. Aurora probably could, but not me, not one of my talents.

He pushed the intercom button and said, "Ryan, swing by my parents' house. I want to check on Jordie." With a "Roger that," Ryan didn't question why his friend would want to check on his daughter, at midnight with a *hot* date by his side.

Jack took my hand and rubbed his thumb across my fingers. "I have to see her."

He needed to make sure his little girl was okay, that she hadn't turned into something he wouldn't recognize. "That's understandable. Do you want to drop me at Harmony?"

"No." He hesitated only briefly. "I don't want our evening to end like this, Tempe. Would you come home with me? After we check on Jordie?"

Was this a good idea, after everything that had

happened? There was only one answer I could give, however, "If you want me…"

"Sweetheart, I've been wanting you since the 17th of February, at about 9:50 am. My world changed then, and that was before any of this other…"

"Bizarre, crazy, unbelievable…"

"Yeah, pick any of those. The morning you delivered that package, I knew my life wouldn't be the same."

"That's a good thing?" I asked.

For a second he didn't answer. "A very good thing." He punctuated that sentiment by pulling me to him and kissing me. The kiss was slow and thorough and had my heart pounding. When it ended, he was leaning toward me, looking at my eyes. "You're eyes change, you know."

I blinked.

His head tilted as he stared at me. "Like that. When the emotion is high, or passion, they have this vortex looking thing going on, like one of those time lapsed videos of stars moving through space. Then they go back to simmering cloudy blue."

"I'm sorry I'm such an aberration." I said, feeling insecure suddenly.

He tipped my chin up so he could stare into my eyes. "Right now, they are as blue as the stratosphere at 30,000 feet." His voice dropped.

"I, uh, don't know what I look like when *it* happens."

"It is pretty strange—" I hit him "—and mind-boggling." He looked at me intently, remembering. "At the Inn, when you were fighting with your dad, there were waves in your hair and ships." I gasped, and he nodded, brows expressive. "*Uh-huh*. It looked like the ocean revealing an entire history of powerful storms, and then you went cyclone, the wind swirling around you so fast it was impossible to distinguish your features. When the boulders started sailing through the air, I had to step in. I was afraid someone would be hurt."

I fiddled with the material in my lap. "The first time, you don't have a lot of control. I remember when River—" Jack's face went white. I said quickly, "It doesn't have to be that way with Jordie. She'll have us to guide her through it. She'll be ready."

"Ready for *what*?" he muttered. "I don't think I'll ever be ready."

Probably more than you know, I thought.

"I wonder what Aurora meant about talking to my parents."

Zeus, Hera and Hades! I wasn't going to touch that one.

CHAPTER 24

TEMPE

I'm not a total moron…

HE DIDN'T WANT me to stay in the car when we arrived at his parents'. No doubt he needed moral support. He must have expected the worst. Beffie met us at the door and we followed him to Jordie's room. She looked like a normal teenager having a restful night sleep. Jack stared at her for several long minutes, his eyes moist when he rose from kissing Jordie on the forehead, whispering, "I love you, baby."

He took my hand and led me back down the hallway, in more of a hurry now that he'd assured himself of his daughter's safety.

I wondered what to expect when we got to his house.

Had he changed his mind about the promise to get me out of my gown, or did he just want a friend?

"What's it like to be a Paramortal?" he asked.

The question caught me off guard. Was I equipped to answer? "I might not be the best one to ask, you know. I went twenty-nine years without owning my heritage, no matter the reason. And I didn't have my family to—what's the best word—to acculturate me to life as a Paramortal. It might be better to ask Dylan or Aurora."

He increased the interior light, listening intently. "I have mixed emotions now, knowing what I do, and I can't help but resent that the truth was kept from me." I turned to him. "No matter what, Jack, *no matter what* reality holds for Jordie, be truthful with her."

He exhaled. "I'm afraid for her. All I ever wanted was for her to be safe, and loved."

"She is loved, Jack. She feels it, and everyone can see the relationship between you is special."

His jaw clenched. "That wasn't always true though. Her mother," he shivered dramatically, "talk about freaks."

"You never talk about…"

"Georgeanne," he sighed. "I don't even like to say her name for fear of conjuring her or something. But back to my question, will this put Jordie in danger?"

I ran the answer through my head before verbalizing it. "I'm not a parent, but I meet a lot of teenagers, and so does Aurora. Jordie seems very mature and well grounded. I understand that to you, she's your 'baby girl' but she really isn't a little girl anymore, Jack. Think about it this way. In about two years, she may decide to follow in your footsteps and enter the military."

"Oh, God." He scrubbed his hands down his face.

"Think of Paramortals as protectors with varying skill sets, many of them are just extra-mortal, not supernatural. We're like the Paramortal Service, except we don't get to retire. Our entire purpose from the time we're born is to defend defenseless humans and others from outside threats. Is that so different from what you've spent all your adult life doing?" The furrows in his forehead deepened. "She might just be a sentinel, or a watcher…"

He held his hand up, "Okay, TMI, as Jordie would say." He sighed, "I get it."

"*Right*. So you're okay with her being a freak like me?"

He smiled, "This is a test, right? I'm not a total moron."

"It's important, Jack," I said, holding his gaze while he considered his answer.

*J*ACK

After Midnight We're gonna let it all hang out.

SHE WANTED MY ACCEPTANCE. I thought I'd already embraced Tempe's supernatural abilities, but the things I'd said had made her question me. I'd been focused on Jordie and not how my comments might hurt Tempe's feelings.

"You are a remarkable woman, Tempest Pomeroy. It's one of the reasons why I'm… why I can't shake my feelings for you." I curled my fingers around hers. "I didn't mean what I said to Aurora—about going back to before I won the election. I was in shock. I'm sorry. Damn, I'm always apologizing to you. Let me explain." I drew put her hand down onto my lap.

"Ever since I got sole custody of Jordie, I've been focused on a narrow set of parameters I felt we had to follow to right the ship so to speak, to fly straight and overcome the past. I had a picture in my head of how that would go."

She chuckled, "Small Town, USA? You sound just like a retired commander."

"What can I say? Pilots and lawmen, we deal in absolutes. It's predictable, dependent on contingencies, backup plans, but controllable. I feel like I've lost control." I palmed her cheek. "But I think I'll get used to it, if I can ever get a few days under my belt to adjust."

Ryan turned the corner and parked in front of my house. I signaled him and he came around to open the door.

"Can I do anything else for you folks this evening?" he asked in his best limo driver voice.

I palmed a bill and shook his hand. "That'll be all, my man. Thanks."

Ryan grinned and slapped me on the back closing the jet door behind us as Tempe started up the driveway, holding her gown off the concrete with both hands. "Tempe," I said softly.

She turned, the full moon reflecting off the stones of her dress. The loose tendrils of her hair floated around her head like a sedate beach breeze version of what I'd seen just two days ago. "Let me..." I scooped her into my arms and carried her to the door.

"My keys are in my left pocket," I said and while she went searching, I nuzzled the smooth perfection of her skin. It was warm and soft and she smelled like some combination of sea breezes and woman. I kissed my way up her throat to nibble on her ear, leaning against the door. A sound escaped her that I took as frustration as she dug for the keys, that part of my pants having suddenly become a tight fit.

I captured her lips as she withdrew her hand, both arms coming back around my neck as she threw herself into the kiss. Her tongue entered my mouth, exploring. Desire sped South. I groaned and attempted to find the keys myself without unlocking our lips. Her hand roamed again, stroked the bulge in my pants, accidentally or not, as she got back to searching for the keys. I locked her in place with one arm, the urge to thrust against her out-weighing the need to get inside.

"Jack," she laughed, and I covered her mouth with mine. I heard a clink, and her hand slipped out of my pocket to clasp my shoulders, her teeth grazing my bottom lip. The kiss became a full on clash of tongues. Keys jangled, which reminded me we were standing on the porch, making out against the front door. Once again, I'd proven that when I touched her I lost track of where I was. I heard the key in the lock. "Jack, wait—okay." The door swung open.

I walked over the threshold and kicked the door shut, struggling to balance with an arm full of fluffy fabric and wriggling woman. "Bolt it," I said with my mouth around her earlobe.

Her breath stuttered, but the lock clicked. Desire nearly slammed me to my knees. Finally, I had her in my house, my arms, this alluring, tempestuous female. I bumped the switch activating the lamp near the couch. Passion stared back at me, her gaze on my lips, her tongue darting out to moisten her own.

I groaned and took her mouth again. I loved kissing her. Her taste was heady, reticent of spice and, "Hmm, you taste good," I said finally releasing her lips and leaning against the inside of the door to get my breath. She flicked her tongue out again, teasing my lower lip.

My pants were cutting off circulation to my lower extremities, one in particular. I moved my hips in an attempt to get more comfortable. I knew what would work, getting us both naked. But I wanted her here, now, against the door. My eyes went to the couch. *Yeah, there, too.* And on the carpet, in front of the fireplace, but first...

I bumped into the back of the couch. Like a siren, she looked up at me and smiled. "Maybe you should put me down."

Reluctantly, I bent to set her feet on the floor. In her heels she stood tall enough that I barely had to look down. "How high are those heels anyway?"

She rolled her eyes. "Six barbaric, excruciating inches."

I leaned forward and ran my tongue along her collarbone. "Then why don't you slip out of them?" I muttered against satiny skin.

She toed the heels off and then her hands slid up my chest to push my jacket off my shoulders. "Need some help with those cufflinks, Commander?"

Tempe

Who cares? am "Please, no lightning bolts."

JACK WASN'T HELPING. "Mmmm, if I do this..." he ran his tongue up the side of my neck making goose bumps form on my arms, pretty good for someone who's never had goose bumps. He pulled back and looked down at me, "I don't have to worry about being electrocuted do I?"

Good question.

His fingers trailed down my chest, dipping into the dress' bodice as his eyes flared. "Your skin is so soft. I want my hands on you."

"Well, then it seems like you'd be more help removing your jacket."

"It's not *my* clothes that are impeding the process, babe. You did look beautiful tonight, but it's time to get you out of that dress."

He placed both hands at my waist and leaned me against the high back of the sectional couch so he could plant kisses on my throat and run his tongue along the swells above the bodice, teasing little quivers from me as his touch caused my breasts to tingle. "Jack..."

He held me with one hand—his arms like steel—and eased the zipper down a few inches. Cool air slid through the opening, as he slipped his fingers inside to put his warm broad hand against my bare skin. "God, you feel so good." He discovered the goose bumps and his head came up. Frowning he asked, "Are you cold?"

I smiled. "Never."

He smiled back. "*Ahh.* You like." His mouth came down on mine. My pelvis rubbed against his groin as his hands roamed to my waist, one cupping my butt through the fabric, the other covering my breast. I squirmed in his arms, trying to get away from the teasing, to get closer to his lips, his hands. He stopped and I saw eyes fierce with need and hot, so hot.

"I want you," I whispered, barely able to speak.

Those were apparently the magic words. He scooped one arm beneath mine and swung me back up into his embrace striding down the hallway with me as if I weighed nothing.

His bedroom was a masculine mix of navy and aqua with dark cherry furnishings. Leaving me standing at the end of the bed, and looking back at me like I was going to run, he shoved the pillows off onto the floor. A man of action, I thought.

Doubts crept in suddenly. What was I thinking? I was so far out of my depth with this man. He was expecting someone with experience, someone he thought was "confident". The dress he'd picked was perfect for that confident, siren of a lover, but not me… I was about to make a fool of myself. I'd only known Jack Lang for two weeks. Granted, we'd been under intense situations where you get to know someone pretty well.

Still, I asked myself, *was this real?* And if it was, what if I screwed it up? I'd thought my feelings for Dylan had been real, but they'd been based on a lie. Everything we'd *been* together had been playacting, body guarding— on his part at least. And I'd been blind to it. *How confusing. Insulting.*

Menori swished her tail. Since when did she pop up during love play? Maybe she meant to remind me that Jack wasn't Dylan. He was honorable, genuine. He probably had some of the same doubts. I wanted him to hold me, to make love with me. But I wasn't like other women he'd known. Now that I'd changed, I didn't know what might happen. He didn't seem to be worried, but I couldn't help it. High emotion for me equaled, well, problems.

CHAPTER 25

Jack

"You're making my eyes cross, sweetheart."

I TOSSED the pillows aside and turned.

Tempe stood at the end of the bed, a deer-in-headlights look in her eyes, as if she was about to turn into a streak of lightning and bolt from the room.

"Sweetheart, are you okay?" Call me crazy, but it seemed I could feel her body vibrating from three feet away.

Her eyes darted to the skylights and her shoulder twitched. "Are you sure about this?"

I shook my head, chuffing a breath. How could she possibly ask? I had an obvious hard-on that was about to split my zipper, and I was practically panting with lust. Not only was I desperate to have her, and I never would have believed this but, I was ready to give our relationship a shot. I hadn't been involved with anyone seriously besides my ex since high school, and that didn't compare to how I felt when I was with Tempe.

I hid none of that from her when I said, "Positive." Her brows lifted. As frustrated as I'd been, as much as I wanted her, I figured I'd have to restrain myself from tearing her clothes off, but the tender feelings I had for her now were new to me. I wanted to go slow. Excruciatingly slow.

"You're making my eyes cross, sweetheart. I tried to talk myself out of this, you know, but I couldn't stop thinking about you, how you make me feel, that I needed to get my hands on your skin, and taste you, every inch of you."

Her eyes went wide as soon as she believed the intensity of my words. The light filtering through the skylights in my bedroom made them sparkle, and I realized her emotions were close to the surface. This could get interesting.

"Stay right there," I said and reached over to open the drapes. "You look beautiful in that moonlight, your hair is even more vibrant; your skin almost translucent. I want you so much, Tempest Pomeroy."

Finally, her eyes glinted and this time it was the look of a seductress. I stepped toward her. She stepped back, and smiled. The brilliant full moon came into view and the lavender-tinted light turned her dress into a blaze of rainbows, darting like gypsy dancers with each of her breaths. Her eyes were starbursts of desire, enticing me, drawing me toward her.

I reached out but she scooted away, "*Uh,uh,uh,*" the seductress warned. "Why don't you sit there on the trunk while I get a little more comfortable."

My eyes widened at the invitation from my surprising temptress. "Whatever you say, darlin'." I sat, leaning back on my elbows. "Go on."

"You know, this could be the most unpredictable night of your life, *Laser,*" she said as she reached around to finish unfastening her dress. Then, holding it to her with just one arm, eyes on mine, she lowered it, one infinitesimally small increment at a time.

My body anticipated, going hard as titanium. My breathing halted as a little more of that rosy iridescent skin was exposed. My mouth went dry when I thought to make her hurry, not that she would have obeyed. The woman was on a mission, to drive me out of my mind. It looked like she might succeed.

Just as her breasts came even with the edge of the ornate bodice, she let her arm fall away and I sighed in anticipation, but some kind of gossamer fabric draped across the swells, a lavender silk so thin it outlined the rosy points of her nipples. I leaned forward...

With one hand she raised her hair off her shoulders, the

movements straining the delicate material, and my zipper, as my mind *wished* it to slip free of whatever was making it remain suspended. With her other hand she shoved the dress off her hips to the floor. I nearly swallowed my tongue.

She was a goddess, her long legs from toes to mid thigh covered in silvery iridescent stockings. And there between her legs, at the vee of her pubic treasure, *that* door was guarded by a tiny triangle of deep violet. She angled her body slightly giving me a different view of one of her bare cheeks and the thin purple piece of silk dividing them—a thong. "*Uhhn…*"

My hand moved to my zipper. I'd never seen anything so sexy in my life. My eyes scanned the length of her body, "I knew you would be magnificent."

Tempe

"What if something bad happens?"

HIS BREATHLESS WORDS sent hot shivers racing down my spine, and I thrilled as he reached out, hooking his finger into the thin strip of the thong, and tugged me toward him. His eyes were the color of the morning mist skimming the bayou, intent, hot with desire, for me, Tempest Pomeroy, Tempestaerie, child of a Djinn. He'd seen me in action and he still wanted me.

His lips covered my breast through the silk of my strapless camisole, loosening it when he nipped the edge with his teeth. One side slid below the tip and he sucked it into his mouth, pulling on the sensitive button, then ravaging my nipples, suckling and tugging, giving them such thorough attention that if my legs would have held me I'd have *endured* it forever. My knees trembled and he straightened, using his hands to angle my head for his kiss, sucking on my tongue, devouring it as if he could inhale me straight into his soul. My eyes opened when his lips left mine, "*Sweet Zeus*! Don't stop."

His shirt abraded my nipples as he turned me around and eased me onto the bed, bending over me to trail kisses along my neck, down a path to where the camisole clung to my hips. His tongue stroked my navel, while one finger teased my entrance, stroked the wetness there, then he added another.

He had but to say my name and I would fly, but I wanted him inside me. He was still dressed. I tugged on his shirt sending three of the tiny pearl buttons flying and pressed my hand to the hard ridges of his stomach. My body was vibrating with need. *Menori* went *off*, singing through my blood like a chorus of stars, light bursting behind my eyes, and electricity tingling through my extremities.

"*Uh*, Tempe, honey?" Jack's voice came from far away. I opened my eyes. He smiled crookedly and looked up at the ceiling. "Think we can we do this without lightning?"

I followed his gaze. Above us, suspended below the

ceiling of the bedroom were tiny crystalline particles, mini prisms of light, water and air, the elemental stuff of Tempestaeries. "It's beautiful," I said reverently. He hadn't moved, but now he reached for my fingers, guiding them into his open zipper.

"You're beautiful," he said. "I wanted to draw this out, but I have to be inside you soon, Tempe."

Fire ignited inside me at his words. I'd never felt more desired. I saw the strain on his face as he tried to hold back.

"I'm afraid, Jack. This…" I waved my arm at the shimmering in the air. "This has never happened before. "What if I lose control, fly apart?" I looked down where my hand was holding his hard length. I looked up into his eyes and swallowed, "What if—something bad happens?"

He kissed me, a sweet tender kiss and said, "What if something beautiful happens?" Another kiss, this time between my breasts. "I've got your six, sweetheart."

Of course he did. It was who he was. If I believed nothing else, I could count on that. I rubbed my hand against his erection, stroked the ridge of flesh that thrummed like one of his Navy jets—thrusting, charged, ready to blast away from the carrier deck. He spread my knees and teased my entrance. "You're ready for me, so hot and wet."

His hands reached under my seat and brought my legs up, the velvety steel prodding my center. His breathing accelerated as I shifted and rolled on top of him, pushing my hips down onto him taking him deep in one sweet slide.

"*Ahh...* sweetheart."

I moved shifting my hips to take him deeper, and deeper still as he thrust rhythmically bringing me into alignment, my breath ratcheted up as the vibrations built within me. "Let go, Tempe, now!" He surged upward and rose with me in his arms. I flew then, sensing when we left the surface of the tarmac and shot into the sky, spinning off into the clouds, the sky darkening and the stars becoming brighter and brighter until I had to close my eyes against the blinding sight, the explosion of fireworks.

I felt the mattress on my back and Jack's forceful thrusts as our bodies slammed against each other, over and over. Then Jack's cry mingled with mine as we twirled, doing a slow spiral back to earth, the sky still dotted with drifting tracers of color.

"Open your eyes, Sweetheart," Jack whispered as if talking too loud would break some spell. My eyes drifted open to look at him. He just grinned, "No lightning, but you sure know how to put on a fireworks display."

"I wouldn't know. I was busy taking another one of your jet rides into space." His eyes crinkled and he nodded at the ceiling once again.

I looked up. My mouth dropped open. It was as if all the particles that had been hanging in the air had exploded, some still bursting like excited sparklers. I couldn't hold back a smile. "Cool, huh?"

He laughed and within seconds we were rolling on the bed like playful puppies. His pants disappeared and a tanned and naked "Six-packs" lay on his back, primed, ready to take me for another ride.

CHAPTER 26

TEMPE

"Another flight to the stars"

MY HANDS GLIDED over the taut pectorals, like smooth flesh stretched over granite. I felt firsthand what I'd heard about a fighter pilot's extraordinary fitness. No inches to pinch here because each muscle in the body needed to be able to respond to the extreme G forces of flight.

His corded thighs flexed against me and the long length of steel between my legs pressed against the entrance of my sex. My fingertips dipped and memorized the ridges of his abs. "How do you stay in this kind of shape?" I asked and moved my hips against that hard shaft.

He gasped. "I… never got out of the habit. It seems to

have gotten easier to stay fit in the last few years though. I don't...*ahh,* really understand it. If you keep doing that..."

"I love having my hands on your skin." I smiled down at him. "I've been fantasizing about it since I saw you on the porch, about how I'd like to see you in nothing but shaving cream." I drew my eyes down over the muscles of his chest and arms, down to where he probed me... "This is better."

His erection got even harder. "Darlin', why don't you hush and climb aboard. Let's see if I can take you on another flight to the stars."

"Do you see it too?" I asked.

He thrust against me. "No, I suspect you're experiencing my memories. It brings back the adrenaline rush, the sites, the excitement. Some flights were *indescribable,*" he grinned, "like making love to you."

I leaned down lifting my hips until the silky tip just grazed my wet sheath. Pleased that I'd been able to let go and enjoy this incredible intimacy with him, I ran my tongue across his bottom lip. His teeth tugged on my lower lip in then his tongue plunged into my mouth sweeping in and pillaging, his hips pumping. I pushed off his chest and slammed my hips down over him.

He was larger than before, filling me to bursting, and I rocked to push his bulk further into my depths. I imagined the tip of his rod touching my heart, like mighty Zeus' spear finding the heart of the Earth. A thunderous crack resonated through my body as I moved faster, meeting his powerful thrusts as our bodies melded and souls converged.

~

JACK

Looks like "faking it" will be out of the question.

THE TERM "fly APART in my arms" took on a whole new meaning. I'd lied to Tempe. My best guess about her hallucinations had been memories of thousands of jet flights and the excitement of revisiting them, but this was more; it was primal; it was unearthly; it was tied to the storm woman I was buried inside. I didn't want our lovemaking to end. I'd felt like this when I flew, suspected it was like doing crack—the rush, the heightened response, the ecstasy.

No, this was more than primal, more than leaving the bounds of the earth. Images of roiling clouds, racing stars and eyes with meteor showers in them preceded a loud *crack*. I felt the lightning bolt between my thighs, heard thunder in my groin, and heat exploded along my shaft as *I claimed this woman for my own.*

She screamed, "*Ah, Jaluu,*" and I knew in my heart, in that part of me that had longed for someone like her who could be my mate, that her soul called to mine. I thought I'd been ready for this, but I'd been as much a virgin as I had as a 15-year-old. Nothing could've prepared me for this—for her.

Her hands dug into my shoulders as she joined the stars or storms or wherever she went. Her skin sparkled like the iridescent light filtering in through the skylights. A distinctive, translucent pink cast was tinting her hair an even deeper red. Her flesh was hot to the touch. I trailed my fingers down over her breasts, cupping them, rising enough to nip at the hot, turgid tips, when my gaze caught on the scraps of material at her hips.

The edges of the camisole she'd worn were charred, the panties as well. Only enough lilac remained that I could identify them. I looked at the mattress below us. There was a ring of fire, and scorched black what-used-to-be-sheets in the outline of our bodies, like a controlled burn at the edge of a wildfire.

A wildfire begun by a lightning strike. It had been real, *not* just my imagination. And I wasn't even singed.

"*Damn*, sweetheart, you give new meaning to the word, 'hot'. You set our sheets on fire."

I pointed to the air flickering, like indoor heat lightning but gradually fading, then down at the bed. "Look's like faking it will be out of the question for you." I grinned.

Her eyes were eerily light, reflecting the moon's luminosity. But her dreamy expression changed when she looked down, and saw the sheets. She whispered, "I'm sorry, Jack." She tried to roll away from me but our bodies were still joined.

"Tempe." She pushed at my chest, and I saw tears on her cheeks. "Tempe. Stop, sweetheart."

Distressed, tear-flooded eyes searched mine. "How can you—"

"*That* was…"

"An aberration?" Her mouth turned down in a defeated grimace. "Bet you never dreamed what it would be like to have sex with a freak." She wiped at her cheek.

I held her wrists firmly but gently when she tried to wiggle free. Her eyebrows drooped as if she expected the worst.

My body quickened once again inside her and her mouth opened as she realized… I wasn't mad, or turned off. *Quite the opposite.* "I'm trying to tell you that it was… Tempe, you have ridden with me in my F-18; experienced G forces; shot up in the atmosphere until you could touch the stars; flew along the water at near supersonic speed and heard the sonic boom. Remember?"

When her mouth curved in a tremulous smile, I knew she was revisiting those flashes of… *love travel? Hooyah!*

I touched my lips to hers, which were swollen from our kisses. I tasted rain and spring and something else that was so exclusively Tempe. Sulfur? Ozone?

I released her lips slowly and my body made its desires known, again. Her eyes widened.

"Don't ask me… never before, *never* have I experienced

anything like this, Tempe. It's like my life, everything I've done, led me to you. To this."

I began moving inside her *again* going deeper with each stroke as she squeezed me with her powerful core, making me even harder, longer. It was as if our intimate parts were feeding off of each other like some internal mating dance. I was awestruck, and totally, mindlessly spellbound when she stopped, and the energy between us began to dissipate. I gasped, "No."

Then I heard her voice, "Jack." My brain cells came back online slowly, her voice making more sense.

"Jack. Someone's at the door."

"Wha—" I sounded drunk. I was. I was intoxicated by this woman who was still impaled on the hardest ride I'd ever had. The noise filtered through. The doorbell ringing—persistently ringing—as if someone was leaning on it. I groaned.

Tempe kissed me, just once and slid to the side. "Sounds, *um*...urgent."

"*Hell.*" I looked at my watch. 3:15 a.m. "Whoever it is, I'm taking my gun."

Tempe giggled, then sobered. "What if it's an emergency?" I could see her tick off all the possibilities with her family and friends in a flash. "Jordie?"

I frowned as the bell continued. "Jordie has a key, I think, and why wouldn't she call? Stay here. I'll check it out," I winked at her, "and get rid of whoever it is."

I threw on my jogging pants. "You don't have to get up."

She walked around the bed and grabbed my robe off the hook on the door. She answered me, hurriedly tying the belt around her waist. "If it's Jordie at this hour, it's important."

I could tell Jack was worried. His mood had gone from sexy and playful to all business in a flash. I wrapped the robe around me, pulled the tie tight and followed him down the hallway. He carefully picked up my dress and draped it over the couch in the living room, then unlocked the door and swung it wide.

"*Nooo*," he nearly growled under his breath and the hand with the gun in it ran through his hair. "*Damn it.*"

CHAPTER 27

TEMPE

"Tell me that wasn't an earthquake... in Louisiana!"

THE PROVERBIAL *BLONDE bombshell* stereotype stood in the doorway. The first thing I noticed were the bright green eyes that looked me over, just before her eyes narrowed. Thick platinum hair fell over her shoulders and impressive cleavage, which was on display for anyone and everyone, the mounds of her breasts nearly spilling out of her lacy low cut blouse, the unbuttoned bodice an unnecessary and obvious contrivance. Her figure was the classic hourglass shape, cinched in tightly at the waist with a silver belt, and she appeared to have been melted and poured into a pair of sequined studded blue jeans. Her lush lips, painted a neon shade of coral, broke into a wide smile.

Jack seemed frozen in place from shock. The woman glanced over his shoulder at me, her eerie green gaze taking in his bare chest, my bathrobe, and the abandoned gown over the back of the couch. "Wow, did y'all feel that? Tell me that was not an earthquake... in Louisiana."

Turning her attention back to Jack, she threw her arms around his neck. "Jack, honey. I'm home."

I felt my eyes widen as my brows nearly met my scalp.

Jack struggled to extricate himself from the blonde.

"Jackie, you haven't introduced me to your... friend." She turned a very controlled show of teeth toward me. "I'm Georgeanne Lang, Jackie's wife—"

"*Ex*-wife," Jack said through clenched teeth. "Tempe, Georgeanne just dropped by, but she won't be staying—"

Her hands clenched around each other, locking him to her. "Oh, now, Jack. Don't be mean." Her voice was like a sly alley cat, slow and sultry, the laser beam green eyes locked on mine. "He's just a bear sometimes, 'ya know? I didn't have anywhere else to go, and I knew he wouldn't turn me away. After all," she tilted entreating eyes up to Jack, "it's been over two years since I've seen my baby."

Did she mean Jordie, or Jack?

Jack tried to push her away but she didn't budge, her hands locked. "Georgeanne, what do you want? Really."

She acted confused by the question. "Why, I just said, didn't I? I missed you and Jordie, so I packed my bags and headed on down to your fine little town." She pronounced "little" with a *lot* of disdain.

"It was nice to meet you Mrs. Lang—" I lied.

"Call me G, dear. Any friend of Jack's and all that..." her insincere show of teeth made me

"I'll leave you to your, um, visit. Jack," I said scooping up my dress.

"Tempe, no." His expression was total horror as he tried once again to shake her loose but it wasn't happening.

I shook my head. *Sorry, Sweetheart.* You'll have to handle this on your own.

Jack's head rolled back against the door frame and he ran his large hand through his hair, mussing it further from what was obviously good-sex bed head. His good mood was gone. He was a man with a giant problem, and I couldn't help him with it.

~

Tempe

Sunday, 3:15am Zeus' darkest night!

ZEUS' darkest night! As I let myself out of Jack's house through the back door I remembered I had no transportation. I could make out the increasingly apparent outline of Cache as it made its trajectory toward the earth moon. It was a pale lavender ghost that would soon obscure the smaller moon and filter out whatever it is that gives us Paramortals our power for at least twenty-four hours. As the coincidence got closer, they would slowly diminish like light from the sun during a total eclipse. Of course, with everything that had happened, I'd forgotten to fill Jack in on details.

How odd was it that Jack's "crazy" ex would show up on the eve of Chaos—as if speaking her name had "conjured" her, his biggest fear. Our personal relationship aside, it was a distraction Jack didn't need. My impression of the green eyed floozie was that she would not go quietly. But whatever the next day would bring, I couldn't make myself fight for a place in Jack's attention. Not tonight. Tomorrow morning would be soon enough.

I wadded up the layers of tulle and crinoline into my arms and started for home. . . on foot.

Grab the next Paramortals book, Eve of Chaos here

But before you go. . .

Find out **how to claim your free** signed reader-exclusive mystery gift - email me liviaquinn@liviaquinn.com
Don't forget to sign up for Livia's spam-free newsletter.

Subscribers will receive exclusive offers, news about new books release and access to special giveaways.
Click here to sign up http://bit.ly/2lJhOB5

For more information:
www.liviaquinn.com
liviaquinn@liviaquinn.com
Facebook Twitter Instagram Amazon Bookbub

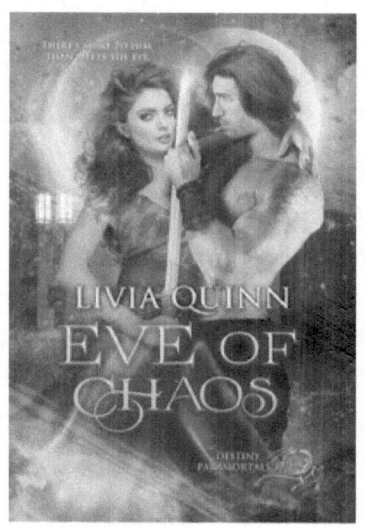

EXCERPT OF *EVE of Chaos*

"That's what I thought," the gnarly-faced creature said. His eyes suddenly burned with hostility, the long door frame incisors and tongue growing larger as the muscles in his body bunched, signaling his attack. He sprang.

Then a hot *whoosh* of flame flashed across Montana's vision. She'd had no time to jump back. As soon as she opened her eyes she realized—*it was over*. A fatal flame had scorched the offending abuser down to his one remaining foot.

Montana and the woman were safe.

Scorch marks marred the floor where the being had stood seconds ago. *Death from above!* Pretty accurate aim. Everything had been annihilated in front of Montana except the woman on the floor and the troll's foot, which was propped on her chest. The victim's one good eye opened and stared at the charred paw inches in front of her. Then her eye drifted toward Montana and and rolled up in her head.

Montana sighed. "Did I do that?" she wondered aloud and looked down her snout at the still oozing tendrils of gray smoke. A deep rumbling—like a hundred Vikings in the great hall enjoying a good joke—came from the direction of the ceiling. She followed the scorch mark up the wall to a blanket of stars against a night sky, and gasped.

The most beautiful creature she'd ever seen towered over her... and the house... with the moons, Luna and Cache', as his artistic backdrop. He leaned against what was left of the roof, dragon smugness—a special kind of arrogance singular to dragons—adorning his features. Well, he had a right to be smug. He'd taken out half the roof and the variant in one fiery exhale, without harming her or the woman on the floor.

"*Oooh*, you're good," she acknowledged, giving him a slight bow. She couldn't find it in her heart to complain about the remaining butt-ugly appendage even though it was probably obstructing the woman's breathing.

He was darker than the night, like a dragon shaped black hole except for his red rimmed snout, eyes and lips which shown like the reflector tape on the emergency vehicles she drove.

"Lassie, you dinnae ken the half o' it. Tell me. What made ye think ye could take on that *hackit* Faerie by yerself in yer lovely wee fog drakon form?"

At least he had a sense of humor. *Hackit* meant *really* ugly. Montana thought about what he'd said. Fog. *Hmm.* "So that's why I couldn't produce the fire..." she said, more to herself. He took her measure intently, his eyes traveling over her lithe ten-foot dragon form. When she changed back to her Valkyrie sized naked warrior body, she thought he smiled.

She stood perfectly still, innately comfortable in her nakedness. A small stream of fire sizzled from his nostrils and the irises swirled in his glowing red-rimmed eyes. His head disappeared from view and Montana felt a pang of disappointment, but he returned with two tiny scraps of fabric. Well, they looked tiny in his massive jaws. He opened his mouth just enough to allow the material to float down and land at her feet. She recognized it—her lingerie. You never knew where they were going to end up when you shifted.

His eyes drifted down lazily, the horny forehead wrinkled as he said, "I know yer secret, Victoria." Who would have thought a forty-foot dragon with a head the size of a house could wink *or* raise a non-existent brow? "Better cover yourself, Lassie. The coppers have arrived."

Order Eve of Chaos

ABOUT THE AUTHOR

Livia moved from D.C. to the wilds of Louisiana where the weather and culture of the region inspired her writing, both her storm faerie, Tempest, *and* her military heroes. She's stored up fodder from her jobs as mail lady, salesperson, plant manager, business owner and professional singer to share with readers. Think of her as her characters' biographer! On the bayou, she is protected from the alligators and bears by her husband and feisty Pomeranian, Dusty.

As they say in my favorite escape, Britain. . .
Caide Mile Failte', A hundred thousand welcomes.
Livia

Contact me here:
liviaquinn.com
liviaquinn@liviaquinn.com

Please Support our troops! It's not a cliché that we owe our veterans our very freedom. Many of our soldiers return with Post Traumatic Stress Syndrome (PTSD), Traumatic Brain Injury (TBI), debilitating injuries and illnesses. Trauma affects the *whole family*.

Veterans Crisis Line call 800-273-8255, press #1
Urgent: Vet needing shelter? Call 1(877) 4AID-VET
Suicide: If you or a loved one has contemplated suicide, call or go online to:
http://www.stopsoldiersuicide.org
Women Veterans Health
Drug Rehab addiction help https://drugrehab.com
Mesothelioma Mesothelioma Navy "Most veterans suffering from a service-related asbestos disease never bother to file a VA Disability Compensation and/or Pension Claim; either because they don't think they are eligible, or simply assume the VA will deny them. "
Volunteer or Donate to help a vet
American Legion (help applying for benefits)
Vet to Vet assistance (a fellow vet helps you w/ info)
https://nvf.org/veterans-request-assistance/

See more on my website Liviaquinn.com